Faerie Spells

The Complete Short Story Series
Books 1-4
Denise D. Young

Sage & Shadows Books

Text copyright 2021 by Denise D. Young.

Published by Sage & Shadows Books.

The Beltane Kiss and *The Faerie Key* previously published in 2016 by Denise D. Young. *The Midnight Path* and *The Cursed Woods* published in 2021.

eISBN: 978-1-956327-01-4

print ISBN: 978-1-956327-00-7

Cover design by Victoria Cooper Art.

Published by Sage & Shadows Books.

The Beltane Kiss
Faerie Spells: Book 1

"And where grows the ring of the faeries, powerful magic sings. And there you'll find the promise of healing, where magic from the earth springs."

—Alexander Finkelstein's Cures and Tinctures for Faerie-Related Maladies

Chapter One

L ily's eyes were unique, a sparkling shade of robin's egg blue. Daisy reminded herself of this—because it had been two months since she'd looked in her sister's eyes. Two months since her sister had laughed in merriment while they drank peppermint tea on the patio overlooking their wild cottage gardens. Two months since Lily had walked downstairs at a leisurely ten a.m., searching for coffee and a blueberry scone.

Daisy remembered the last day she'd spoken to her sister. It had been a surprisingly warm Virginia spring evening.

They'd just finished stockpiling their homemade teas and bath products for the farmers' market where they hawked their wares, and Daisy had suggested a twilit stroll in the forests surrounding their ramshackle farmhouse.

That had been the last night Daisy had seen Lily as she was meant to be—laughing, gleeful Lily. By the time midnight fell, Lily had slipped into a troll-dust induced sleep from which she'd yet to awaken.

Now, on the evening of Beltane—May Day, as it was also known—Daisy might have a chance at ending the troll dust's curse once and for all.

She squeezed her sister's hand, cold despite the room's warmth.

"I found a cure," Daisy whispered, hope fluttering its feathered wings in her belly.

Maybe the next time the sun rose, Lily's eyes would be open. Maybe then life could begin again, brush away this period of waiting and mourning.

Daisy swept Lily's brown locks away from her face and rose, grabbing the basket she'd set on the nightstand, next to a vase of lilies and a milk-glass lamp.

By the time she returned, she vowed, she would have a cure. And this waiting would be at an end.

RHETT SPIED THE TRESPASSER just as the sun was slinking behind the hills.

No. Why tonight, of all nights? Why on Beltane, when the fae were at their most deadly?

She was a wisp of a thing, this forbidden visitor in the May twilight.

A waterfall of chestnut hair cascaded down her back. She wore a pair of faded jeans and a white peasant top, a basket tucked under one arm. A wisp, indeed—not more than five feet tall, her body lithe and slender.

And she was on his land.

A flash of familiarity shot through him. He'd seen her before—but where?

He recalled one of the recent fundraisers he'd been to, a dinner for the local farmers market. She'd been there, clad in an inky blue sundress and strappy sandals. A wave of heat coursed through him. She was a beauty. But she still didn't belong here, he thought with a growl.

Rhett Fairshadow set his smartphone down on the table, the email he'd been sending to his financial advisor tabled for the moment.

It was less that he cared about the trespassers and more that he worried what they would run into. The fae were ruthless, and nowhere was their presence stronger than in the Fairshadow woods.

And so he had a role to play.

When he wasn't spelunking or kayaking, he was the stereotypical wealthy recluse, emerging only a few times a year to attend the requisite fundraising dinners. So, as far as the residents of Foster Springs were concerned, he should've had no reason to care that this young woman was wandering the grounds of Fairshadow Manor, as though she were Little Red, off to visit her grandmother.

Except that he knew something most people didn't. Faeries were real. And they were not your friend.

There were always pockets, places where the veil between the worlds was thin. And nowhere was that veil thinner than at Fairshadow Manor. The grounds were on a nexus of sorts, a powerful place where fae came to dance and play. And woe to any unsuspecting human caught in their path. They didn't like human trespassers.

Rhett's own reputation as a grouchy recluse kept most trespassers at bay. Emphasis on most.

So, who was this woman, and what in the gods' names was she doing frolicking across his property?

Rhett muttered a few choice words under his breath as he slipped on a pair of hiking boots. He sure as hell wasn't dressed for a hike, but he had to find this woman. He had to send her away before it was too late.

There might have been friendly fae out there, but the ones Rhett had met were vicious. And they hated humans. They'd eat this poor woman for dinner.

She was heading into the heart of the wood that surrounded the manor house.

The house, built by his grandfather in a neo-gothic style, had a foreboding façade of gray stone complete with gargoyles and high-pitched eaves. The manor was a warning; *do not enter*, the very architecture seemed to scream.

Clearly this woman wasn't getting the message.

He grabbed a battery-powered lantern and slipped out the back door into the twilit sky, deep blue mixed with a vivid sea of reds and oranges.

The fog was already rolling in, as it did every night. The mystical energies of the place seemed to demand it.

Here, time stopped. It might have been the thirteenth century instead of the twenty-first.

The mansion's neo-gothic stone façade was foreboding in the gloaming. And, to be honest, he liked it that way.

There was a side of himself he loathed, a side he ran from—and he wasn't one to shrink from a challenge.

But the fae blood that coursed through his veins, and the accursed land on which his family estate sat, reminded him how little he fit into the human world. Part human, part fae.

And hadn't Miranda reminded him of that unforgettable distinction as she'd walked out the door, stomping on his heart a few times for good measure on the way out?

But there wasn't time to travel down that rabbit hole of memories tonight. His unwanted visitor was already in the wood. Damn.

He followed, hoping beyond hope that he wasn't too late.

THE WOOD SMELLED OF damp earth, ferns, and mushrooms.

In short, exactly what Daisy needed.

It was here that she would find what she was looking for. The one thing that might save her sister.

If the ancient text she'd found was true, then it was here, in a wild wood, on the night of Beltane, under the moonlight, that she would pick the mushrooms of a faerie circle.

Then, she would string them to hang above her sister's bed. The mushrooms, charged with faerie magic, would draw out the poison.

And then, maybe, Lily would wake up—her old self again.

Daisy remembered better days. Days when her sister's blue eyes glimmered with mischief. Sunny summer afternoons when Lily could make even the dullest of chores lively.

They'd laughed as they hung the laundry on the land. They'd laughed over Chinese take-out while they'd paid the bills for the creaky old farmhouse they shared. They'd sung songs while weeding their garden.

But two months had passed since the incident, and Daisy was beginning to wonder if things would ever be the same.

For now, Lily lay like a stone statue in her four-poster bed. Her once-sparkling eyes were now dull and blank. Her lips couldn't form a smile or sing a pleasant tune.

For the last two months, Daisy had scarcely slept. She'd traveled up and down the East Coast, combing through troves of information about poisoning by troll dust.

Finally, last week, she'd discovered an old, leather-bound book titled *Alexander Finkelstein's Cures and Tinctures for Faerie-Related Maladies*. And this—these mushrooms, plucked from a faerie ring—was the answer, his text had assured her.

And at no time of year was faerie magic more accessible than on Beltane—or so her reading told her.

So here she was.

Because she'd heard a rumor, the kind those old souls who still believed the even older tales whispered to those willing to listen.

There is magic in the wooded hills of Fairshadow Manor. Faerie magic.

Her elderly neighbor, Eudora Cooper, had been the one to tell Daisy about Fairshadow Manor.

"We share these woods," Eudora had said one night as they sipped sweet tea on her front porch. She rocked her chair back and forth and gazed into the forests beyond the fields of grazing cattle.

"We ain't alone and ain't never been. And you want to know where the fae roam wilder than anywhere else? It's at the land of that peculiar young man—young Mr. Fairshadow. His family's always had dealings with the fae. You want to save Miss Lily, you seek your answers there." And then, with a firm nod of conviction, she'd sipped her tea.

Though Daisy had lived in Foster Springs for two years—since she and Lily inherited the farm and tea business from their Great-Aunt Marigold—she'd only seen Rhett Fairshadow once, the year before at a benefit for the farmers market.

She remembered him as gruff and reserved—and far grumpier than his twenty-eight years seemed to warrant. She remembered long blond hair pulled back in a careful ponytail, silvery eyes that peered out at her.

A shiver of remembrance swept over her.

Gorgeous, yes. And impenetrable? That, too.

She tore her thoughts away from Fairshadow Manor's reclusive owner.

She just had to find a faerie circle, pluck the mushrooms and tuck them safely into her basket, and then she would be on her way.

She could only hope that the faeries here didn't notice her—and that neither did the grumbling manor owner.

Twisting shadows crept across the wood, shrouding it in a misty darkness, so she pulled the flashlight out of her basket and flicked it on. She was far enough from the manor that its owner shouldn't see the light if he happened to look out a window. She only hoped she could find a faerie ring before the mists grew any thicker.

She pointed the light at the forest floor and began her search, methodically scanning each area for a ring of mushrooms.

"What in Lucifer's name do you think you're doing?" a voice behind her growled. She almost jumped out of her skin.

She spun around to find Rhett Fairshadow, the "lord of the manor" himself, glaring at her, a picture of annoyance.

How was it she hadn't heard his approach? Was he silent as a panther, or was she simply too caught up in her search to hear his footfalls?

"I..." She knew she couldn't possibly tell him the truth.

Rhett's silvery-gray eyes bored into hers. His blond hair was tied back in a simple ponytail, a contrast to his crisp white cotton shirt and khakis.

She adjusted her grip on the basket. The truth was not an option. Who would believe such a far-fetched story? Some days Daisy wasn't sure she believed it herself.

Most of the residents of Foster Springs, Virginia, didn't believe in the fae. They made up all sorts of far-fetched, yet somehow more mundane reasons, for the strange happenings in the forests around town—rabid coyotes, chemical spills, roving bands of rabble-rousers—anything to keep at bay the truth that the fae roamed these forests.

"Cat got your tongue?" he sneered. "Get off my land before I call the cops and have them escort you to jail for trespassing." He leaned forward, as if trying to drive the point home.

She sucked in a breath, and she caught the scent of cloves and mint. Not an unpleasant combination. Jail? For collecting mushrooms? That seemed a little harsh.

"All right," Daisy said. Best to feign innocence, after all. "I'll just be on my merry way."

Truthfully, she had no intention of leaving without those mushrooms. She'd have to come back later when the lord of the manor, his royal crankiness, was asleep.

He stood there, glaring at her in the lantern light, arms crossed over his chest, electric lantern dangling from one hand. He glowered. Actually glowered. The moon's crescent sliver shone down on them, complementing the already silvery hue of his eyes.

No. There was no time to think of Rhett Fairshadow's eyes of liquid silver, or to wonder what his face would look like with a smile lit across it. And yes, she wondered.

Heat pooled in her stomach. She remembered him in his pale blue dress shirt and black tie at the dinner. When they'd met, yes, the vaguest of smiles had crossed his lips. The heat in her gut coalesced into a ball of desire. They'd merely shaken hands, but the merest touch had sent sparks tingling through her body.

Lily had teased her, Daisy remembered. *You want the laird of Fairshadow Manor*, her sister had joked.

The laird. Only Lily.

Lily. Daisy had to think only of her sister. Guilt niggled at Daisy's gut. It was her fault that Lily had been poisoned.

He didn't stop staring. He crossed his arms across his chest and waited.

Wordlessly, she turned toward the driveway to the manor, to her car, which she'd parked on the side of the wending lane lined with a low stone wall. The wall was no doubt supposed to be a hint. Stay away.

She couldn't bring herself to care. In the past two months she hadn't come this close to a cure. Damned if she would wake the next day without one.

He walked her through the wood and across a field, to where her trusty blue sedan was parked in the shade of a towering oak.

After she hit the unlock button, he opened the door for her without saying a word. The formal gesture surprised her.

He was a strange mix of brooding and formality. She climbed in, muttering an awkward thanks that mixed together with an apology, even though she wasn't sorry she'd come, only that she'd been caught.

And there he stood until she got in the car, turned the key, and made her way back down the road. She felt his hot gaze on her back as she drove away, and it sent tingles down her spine long after she was out of his line of sight.

She stopped at the end of the drive and put the car in park, sure she was far enough away that he could no longer see her car or taillights.

And there, she waited.

Chapter Two

It was half past eleven p.m. when Daisy decided to brave the forested hills of Fairshadow Manor again.

This time she hiked all the way from the road, worried Rhett Fairshadow would catch a glimpse of her headlights. The trek was long, and she was grateful she'd donned a sturdy pair of hiking sandals. She entered the wood again and started her search anew.

The flashlight's beam glinted off a yellow sign: *Posted. No trespassing.* She ignored it. She had to. This was her only shot to save her sister, and Daisy wasn't giving up.

Soft earth padded her footfalls. The scent of evergreens and mushrooms tickled her nose as she arced the beam from left to right, searching for a faerie ring.

A sound made her stop.

Strains of music reached her ear, as wild and haunting as a wolf's howl. The music was discordant and fey, and it told her one thing: Faeries were nearby.

The hairs on the back of her neck stood up. Her last run-in with faeries had ended with Lily's poisoning by troll dust. Daisy wasn't looking forward to another face-to-face with the "wee ones."

The music rose, the pluck of a lute, the enthralling sound of pan pipes rising in the night, seeming to draw the very moon down from her perch in the sky.

Daisy stopped as the beam caught a circle of mushrooms. She knelt and examined them. A perfect circle. This was it. Her search was over. She'd found the faerie ring.

She set her basket on the forest floor and began to pluck the mushrooms one by one, placing each one gingerly into the basket. Tonight she'd string them above Lily's bed and surround her with clear quartz crystals to draw out the poison.

And who knew? Maybe tomorrow she'd hear Lily's laughter again, the way it bubbled out of her like a babbling brook, clear and sweet.

The farmhouse, a turn-of-the-century house inherited from a very eccentric elderly aunt, felt haunted and empty without her sister's mirth. A hush had fallen over the house, from the dining room where they hung herbs to dry from the rafters to the kitchen where they packaged their herbal teas and baked blackberry tarts.

She placed the last of the mushrooms in her basket and rose, brushing dirt off her jeans and tucking the basket once more in the crook of her arm.

Now, if only she could get back to her car without Fairshadow spotting her again, she'd be in the clear.

"I'm coming, Lil," she whispered to the still night air.

A breeze ruffled the leaves. A giggle sounded nearby, the sound childlike, yet somehow menacing.

"Who's there?" Daisy said, shining the beam of the flashlight in arcs around her. She spun in a complete circle, and yet she saw nothing.

And then it approached. It appeared to be a child of no more than six or seven, but Daisy knew better. This was a faerie—one of the changelings, to be precise. They could pose as children, but the heart of a monster beat in their chests.

Daisy shuddered. The thing tiptoed toward her.

"Pretty lady. Why are you out in our woods?" it asked. Stringy blond hair framed a misshapen face. Its buggy green eyes were too large, like those of a terrifying doll. Its fingers ended with sharp talons. The curved claws of its bare feet scratched the dirt. It smiled wickedly, revealing teeth that came to sharp points.

Daisy shivered. The changeling rushed her, and she screamed. The basket fell out of her hands, its fall cushioned by the forest floor. The mushrooms she'd so carefully collected lay scattered on the ground.

"No!"

The changeling lashed out with its talons, scratching Daisy's face and leaving a searing series of gashes. She reached up and felt the warm rush of blood against her fingers.

"Take you home. Be my pet," the changeling hissed.

Two more changelings emerged from the bushes, each as misshapen as the first. Their eyes seemed to glow in the night, haunting shades of amber and citrine.

The first one grabbed her wrist, causing her to drop the flashlight. It hit the ground and its light vanished. Only then did Daisy realize how comforting the tiny swath of light had been.

These woods were truly wild. She hadn't known how much until just that moment.

The changelings circled and then she heard the scrape of talons against tree bark.

She didn't have time to wonder what that scraping sound meant.

A changeling came flying out of the canopy, landing on her chest and sending her crashing to the ground so hard the air left her lungs.

FOOLISH WOMAN.

The scream he'd heard could only mean one thing: she'd waited until he'd fallen asleep and then snuck back onto his land.

Every curse word Rhett could think of pounded in his head as he slipped on a pair of jeans and running shoes and snatched his electric lantern from the hook by the back door. He tucked an iron dagger into the sheath on his belt, ignoring the sting of the metal against his skin.

It wouldn't leave a scar the way it would if he were pure fae. But he had enough fae blood in his veins for the iron to burn.

It was the middle of the night. What was wrong with her? What could possibly be important enough to sneak onto his land twice in one night?

And now, no doubt, the faeries had her.

Worry hit him like a punch to the gut.

He pictured those eyes like blue topaz, that lavender-scented chestnut hair through which he longed to run his fingers.

He pictured her, scarred or maimed or worse, all light leaving her glistening eyes.

Yes, he was drawn to her, moth to the flame and all that jazz.

But that didn't matter now. All that mattered was keeping her safe—a task at which he had so far failed.

Damn the fae. Curses resounded in his head as he bolted toward the forest.

Why had she come back? Why couldn't she stay away, safely tucked into her home, away from the fae?

Gods knew the fae weren't exactly Tinkerbell. They could be mischievous, but they could also be cruel.

And now his unwelcome guest was about to experience their cruelty firsthand.

Drums beat in the night, a wild frenzy calling up to the sky. The fae reveled tonight, in their own wild fashion marking the turning of the Wheel of the Year, and May Day. He felt their presence every day, but on certain days the place overflowed with fae—and this day was one of those.

Rhett followed their music to the top of the hill, shutting off his lantern and allowing the dim light of the waxing moon to light his path. He kept to the tree line, surveying the situation.

They'd erected a massive bonfire around which faeries of all shapes and sizes reveled. There were trolls, not more than three feet tall with warted skin and stocky builds. There were gnomes, not more than a foot high, with their beards and pointed hats. Changelings danced, too, their forms made all the more monstrous by their hideous countenance.

He spotted a dryad with branches for hair, her skin the texture of birch bark. And then there were the Fair Folk themselves, tall and proud, their skin pale, their eyes gleaming.

Rhett brushed his long blond hair behind his ear and scanned the scene, seeking.

Then he saw her, tied to a tree at the edge of the clearing where the revelry took place. She was tied tight, squirming against her bindings, her chestnut locks wild and wind-blown.

One of the changelings held a stick in the flames, waited until it caught fire, and then pressed it to her feet, which were now bare. She screamed and writhed.

He couldn't wait to devise a plan. He had to act.

THROUGH TEAR-BLURRED eyes she saw Rhett leap out from the surrounding forest, a dagger glistening in his hand.

The flames of the bonfire flickered, taunting her. Her feet ached, blistered from where the changeling had pressed a bit of Beltane flame to her bare skin. Even her throat was dry now, parched and aching.

Rhett didn't have to come for her. But there he was. His eyes shone fiercely in the moonlight, as he dared the fae to do battle with him. His hands were clenched white-knuckle around a dagger's hilt.

Iron. It had to be. That was the only thing that could make the fae give him the berth they were giving him, the only thing that could cause the torch to tremble in the changeling's hand.

Rhett brandished the weapon, swiping it in circles around him.

He'd come for her. Daisy struggled against the rough rope that bound her hands, ignoring the way it cut into her flesh, trying to squirm her way out of the bonds. But it was no use.

"Leave here, human. This is our place. This is our night," said a fae woman with branches for hair, her voice like the tinkling of bells.

"Not without her," Rhett growled.

He glanced in Daisy's direction, his eyes dark as storm clouds, and something jumped inside of her, something she couldn't explain. Why had he come for her? He should've left her to her fate, had no reason to race to her rescue. And yet there he was. Stupid, stupid man.

One of the changelings pointed at her and hissed. "Trespasser."

"On *my* land. Leave her to me," he said, allowing a jagged edge into his voice.

"It is our land tonight. You remember the accords," said a tall fae man with silvery locks and eyes as pale and blue as winter starlight.

Daisy was in too much pain to wonder what the accords were, to question whatever strange relationship existed between Rhett Fairshadow and the fae. Clearly, it wasn't an amiable one.

The changeling passed the torch from hand to hand. *Not again*, she wanted to beg, but she refused. The fae had taken two months of her sister's life—and who knew, maybe whatever days Lily had left, if Daisy didn't find a cure. The fae had taken an innocent walk in the woods and turned it into something sinister, and for that she would never forgive them.

"Let me take her with me and continue your celebrations without your prisoner," he said, as if trying to reason with them.

There was no use. One did not simply reason with the fae. That much she knew.

The changeling who wielded the makeshift torch tossed it into the fire and approached him, and she breathed a temporary sigh of relief. The creature eyed the blade nervously. But it leaned toward his face and hissed, "Never. She is ours."

"No," Rhett said. Something flashed in his eyes, like moonlight glinting off a mirror. And then he sprang.

He grabbed the changeling—no easy feat, as she knew firsthand the creature was strangely strong despite its small frame. It was all bone and muscle, and its lithe body writhed under the pressure of his grasp. He held the creature with its back to him and pressed the blade to its throat. A collective gasp ran through the other fae.

"She leaves with me, or your life is forfeit." He gestured to the silver-haired faerie. "Untie her."

The fae man eyed him, blue eyes narrow, as if deciding whether to call his bluff. Finally, he nodded, and one of the other changelings approached Daisy and cut her bindings. She stood, wanting nothing more than to flee the fae-infested forest.

She bit her lip so hard she tasted blood. The gashes on her face from the changeling's claws burned. Her wrists were raw from the rope, and the pressure on her scorched feet was almost too much to bear.

But there was no time to bemoan her fate. They had to get out of here before the fae turned the tables on them.

She hobbled to Rhett's side. He swept her up into his arms, and without a word, carried her into the forest.

"Rhett Fairshadow," a hissing voice called behind them. "Remember."

An angry cackle followed them into the woods, half war-cry, half pure rage.

Daisy shivered and leaned into Rhett's warmth.

Once they'd gotten far enough away, he glared down at her.

"There is a reason," he said, grinding out each word angrily, "That I tell people to stay away. Do you understand that?"

She blinked back tears and bit her lip again, her feet throbbing. "I had my reasons."

Could she trust him with the truth? Surely he would understand wanting to save her sister.

Rumors swirled that his heart was cold as stone, that it had been broken once and could love no more.

Sometimes rumors were true.

But he'd come racing to her rescue, so maybe, as was often the case, this particular rumor was not.

Chapter Three

R hett didn't utter another word as he carried her back to the manor. With its gray facade, it looked like something out of a medieval village, the architecture almost deliberately out-of-place in the small Virginia town.

He opened a side door that led into a state-of-the-art kitchen, stainless steel appliances and granite countertops gleaming. Daisy choked back tears. Her feet ached from the changeling's torch and from the walk through the forest to the manor.

He sent her down gently, and the tile floor was welcomingly cool under her blistered skin.

"How are your feet?" he grumbled. His gaze bored into hers, intense, penetrating.

Something about that gaze—somehow heated and worried at the same time—gave her pause. She'd never thought she would be at Rhett Fairshadow's mercy.

Did she dare to tell this man the truth about her sister?

"Sore," she admitted.

He closed the distance between them. His large hands encircled her waist, and for an instant she leaned against him, inhaling his masculine scent, her messy brown locks tumbling against his now t-shirt-clad chest.

He lifted her up onto the counter and pushed up the bottoms of her jeans. He flipped on some recessed lighting above the counter and inspected the damage.

"You're lucky." Again, a grumble, but somehow it had lost its edge.

"I don't *feel* lucky," she countered.

He grabbed a dishrag, wet it in the sink and pressed its icy coldness against first one foot, then the next. She winced at the first contact, and then breathed a sigh of relief as the cool water helped the worst of the sting to fade.

"It could've been worse." His eyes locked onto her injured feet, as though he didn't want to make eye contact with her. "They were playing with you. If I hadn't heard your scream..." His voice trailed off.

She pressed a hand to his muscled shoulder, a rush of warmth trailing down her arm. "Thank you, Rhett. You are a good man."

He grunted in response, seeming almost...vulnerable, perhaps? He was a modest man, that much she could tell, though perhaps wanting in the social skills department.

She thought of what she knew about him. Wealthy. Aloof. Thrill-seeking—he always seemed to be off to some far-flung corner of the country or the world, scaling a mountain or camping miles and miles away from civilization.

Somehow, in that moment, she questioned everything she knew about him.

"Can you make it to the living room? You'll be more comfortable in there," he said, rising and dumping the dishcloth into the sink.

"Yes. I'll manage," she said quietly.

He led her through the kitchen and down a hall, to a large room with a fireplace above which hung a big-screen TV. A leather sofa and matching brown leather club chairs sat in a se-mi-circle around an oversized glass coffee table.

The chandelier's light glinted off the unblemished surface of the glass coffee table. She sat on the modern leather sofa and stretched her legs out.

He stood in front of her. Slowly, as if uncertain, he reached down and brushed her hair away from her cheek. "They got you good, didn't they?"

The gashes on her cheek. She'd nearly forgotten. Surprised by his touch, she could merely nod.

He left and returned with a first-aid kit. He opened the red box and tore an antiseptic wipe out of its package. He sat beside her, his knee bumping hers. She caught a whiff of his scent again, cloves and mint, and she inhaled deeply.

He pulled back, the wipe covered in dark red streaks of dried blood. "Am I hurting you?"

She shook her head a little too vigorously, feeling her cheeks turn pink. "It's okay." Her throat constricted around the words, and they came out a little too high and rushed.

"Tell me why you came here," he instructed, and the command was the gentlest she'd heard him speak.

He grabbed a tube of ointment and swabbed it onto the cuts on her cheek. He turned away from her, and she caught him rubbing some of it onto his hands. Had he been injured in the skirmish with the fae?

She took his wrist, spun him toward her. "What's wrong?"

She examined his hands, red and swollen with a couple blisters on each palm. "What happened?"

He drew his wrist out of her grasp and turned away from her. "It's nothing. I picked up a cast-iron skillet, forgot it was hot. Stupid thing to do, I know." The words came slightly too fast.

Why did he feel he had to lie to her? she wondered, but she let it go. If he didn't want to open up, she wouldn't push.

He closed the first-aid kit and set it on the coffee table. "Would you like something to drink? I have this tea my buyer purchases for me at the local farmers' market."

"From Tea Thyme?"

"Yes. You know it?"

"I own it."

He walked over to a bar and bustled around. He turned on an electric kettle and grabbed a canister out of a cabinet.

"Now, you mind telling me why you're here?" he said. "Especially after I kicked you off my land once." He must've recognized his harsh tone because to her surprise, he looked chagrined. "I'm sorry. My people skills are...well, somewhat nonexistent."

"You're much more comfortable threatening faeries with iron weaponry?"

"How did you know it was iron?"

"I'm not a neophyte in the world of faerie lore."

"And yet you came to their stomping grounds on Beltane," he grumbled as he spooned loose leaf tea into two strainers and placed them in squarish white mugs.

"I had no other choice," she said.

"I'm still waiting for that explanation."

She crossed her arms over her chest. "You want an explanation? Fine. Two months ago my sister and I decided to go out for a moonlit stroll. We'd gone deeper into the forest than we'd ever dared. Two trolls leapt out from the shadows, and, when they learned we had no jewels or gold to give them, they hit my sister with troll dust and left her for dead. They said her suffering would be our payment."

A wave of all too familiar guilt swept over Daisy. That walk had been her idea. And Lily had paid the price. "I've found a cure, but it involved gathering the mushrooms of a faerie circle at night. And the magic is strongest at the cross-quarters. I couldn't wait. I don't know how much longer she can go on."

His face softened. He was handsome, to be sure—even more so when he wasn't grimacing or snapping. His face was so chiseled it could've been made out of marble, and the tight fit of his t-shirt suggested an equally chiseled physique.

She pushed the thought aside. It didn't matter. What did matter was saving her sister.

She rose, ignoring the stinging pain in feet. "Look, I need to go back to the forest and collect the mushrooms I dropped. Don't worry. I won't bother you again."

He stepped into her path, his large frame dwarfing hers. He placed his hands on her shoulders. "You'll be toast for sure if you go back out into those woods before dawn. This is *their* time."

She stepped out of his grip. "As I explained, I don't have a choice."

The electric kettle beeped, and he poured them each a cup of tea. "Drink this first," he said. "You have to understand what's just happened."

He handed her a mug and took his, settling into the chair closest to the sofa. He brushed his blond hair away from his face. His brow creased. "The fae view this land, more than any other place in Foster Springs, as theirs," he said. "So my family made a treaty with them, to keep the Fairshadows safe. I've broken the treaty by interrupting the faerie's sacred gathering. Now they are free to come toward the house."

"I'm sorry. I didn't realize." Unsure what else to say, she took a sip of tea. She tasted chamomile, red clover, lemon balm, and lavender. She recognized it as the calming blend they sold at the farmers' market. It had been one of many recipes in Aunt Marigold's handwritten recipe book.

He drank his tea and stared into the darkened fireplace. "I'm not the man everyone thinks I am." The words were laced with bitterness, and her heart lurched.

"No one thinks you're a bad person, Rhett. Just a bit...well, eccentric." She winced at the lie. She'd heard people say less than kind things about him.

He snorted. "I may be many things, but a fool I am not." He met her eyes. "What's your name?"

"Daisy McAllister."

"Well, Daisy, I admire your courage, but I can't send you back out into those woods." He stared into his tea cup before glancing back up at her. His eyes were dark as a sky heavy with the promise of spring rain. "I'll do it."

"No!" She reached out, wrapped her fingers around his muscled arm, heat slithering under her skin. "You can't. If I read the spell correctly, I must be the one to gather the mushrooms. It can't be secondhand."

His gaze locked onto her vice-like grip on his arm, and she reluctantly withdrew her hand. The still air felt somehow cold away from the warmth of his body. She clenched her fingers. "You can't..."

"I know." The words came out tight, a mere whisper. She wouldn't be defeated. "I have to." She rose, ignoring the pain in her feet. It didn't matter. Lily mattered.

She set her half-drunk tea on the coffee table and brushed past him. Maybe she would be faerie fodder if she went into those woods, but she couldn't just sit here and drink tea until the sun rose.

Rhett caught her arm. "Daisy, look at me." The way his tongue caressed her name sent a shiver down her spine and gave her pause.

No one had ever said her name like that before, with such arresting tenderness. She met his eyes. She was greeted with kindness and understanding—and not the pity Lily's condition usually elicited.

He rested the back of his hand against her uninjured cheek. "There might be another way," he said.

Rhett set his mug on the glass coffee table, amid a brass candleholder shaped like a branch and a neatly fanned pile of magazines, almost all of them related to the outdoors. He stared out the window into the moonlit yard, and she studied him. Why did he hold himself apart? Would he ever let anyone in?

She pictured her sister's ashen face. Once tan from working in the gardens and taking long walks, Lily's face was now ghostly. Her eyes that once danced with mirth were now closed and empty. Daisy cleared her throat. "What is it?" she asked. If there was another way, she had to know now.

He continued staring out the window and she thought, perhaps, that he simply ignored her. But finally he spun around.

"The fae can sense human energy in the forest. And the nexus here amplifies that power. It's one reason I'm so, er, strict about trespassing."

Ah. How alone he must feel, wandering around a mansion surrounded by fae and too afraid to let anyone in.

She approached and reached toward his face, wanting to brush those long silky blond strands away from his tanned cheek. "I understand now."

"There is one way. I have a...a bit of magic. Perhaps it will be enough to call the mushrooms to us."

It was her turn to gaze into the moonlit yard, unsure how to respond. "Magic? What sort of magic?"

"Just a little magic that I can summon when necessary. A little spell, here and there. It might not be enough to call the mushrooms to us. But it just might work."

Her head was beginning to ache. Faeries cavorting on Beltane night. Mushrooms that some aged text said could save her sister's life. A mysterious recluse who claimed to have magical abilities.

She was hardly surprised by anything anymore, numbed to whatever mystical revelation came about next.

Moonlight caressed the gardens outside Fairshadow Manor. In a few hours, the sun would rise. By then the mushrooms' magic would be too weak to be of use.

"Let's try it," she said. She didn't know what else to say.

He nodded. "This way."

HE LED HER THROUGH the finished basement, which included motion-activated lights, a gym complete with a rock-climbing wall, a meditation room and yoga studio, and a sauna. It was his sanctuary.

Going out into the company of strangers could be exhausting. He always seem to come off harsher, more standoffish than he wanted, and his fae side always meant his senses were on high. Every woman doused in perfume, every man who seemed to have swum in cologne assaulted his senses.

Except Daisy. Daisy smelled like clothes dried in the sunshine, freshly baked bread, and a hint of lavender. There was something down-to-earth and comfortable about her, something that pleasantly stirred his senses and set his mind at ease at the same time.

She was unique.

So, tonight he would call upon the small bit of magic that flowed through him, and then he would resign himself to seeing her at fundraisers. How could he ever ask anything more?

Miranda had taught him that, while his money was appealing, nothing else about him was. Not his stiff demeanor at dinner parties. Not his freakish fae nature. Not the fact that he'd rather hike in the remote Rockies than sip espresso in bustling streets of Paris.

This basement...this space was his respite. Here he didn't think of faerie dealings or what others thought of him. Here he lost himself, finding his edge and pushing it a little further each time.

He led her through a door to the outside.

They emerged in a small garden with flagstone walkways, surrounded by a low stone fence.

"The fence is fortified with iron," he explained.

None of the fae dared enter the small space, and the iron in the fence wasn't enough to harm him. His hands were always covered in blisters after handling iron. It couldn't kill him like it could the fae, but extended direct contact still burned. He'd tried gloves, but they were of little use.

They followed a pathway that spiraled around and around. At the center was a water-filled stone basin doused in moonlight. Stars twinkled above, and the clear, liquid surface reflected them back like a looking glass.

He closed his eyes and breathed in, feeling the tingle of magic under his skin. He hadn't done magic in years—wanted little to do with it, quite frankly.

But there was something vulnerable and yet determined about Daisy McAllister. Something that made him want to help her. Something that made him want to let her in.

She already knew about the magic. How would she react if she knew about his fae lineage? The fae had harmed her sister—had tortured Daisy tonight. He wouldn't blame her if she learned his secret and bolted, never to be heard from again. It wouldn't be the first time.

He'd only let one person in. His ex-fiancée, Miranda. She'd gotten one good look at the *real* Rhett Fairshadow and bolted. As in, packed up her stuff and left, never to be seen in Foster Springs again.

But what was Daisy to him? Nothing. A mere stranger. So what would it hurt to tell her?

Worst case, she blabbered on about it to the whole town, and the only ones who would believe her were children who still believed in fairy tales and the old ones who clung fast to their superstitions. So what did it matter, really?

Oh, it mattered. He wasn't sure how or why, but it mattered.

He lit the torches that surrounded the circle. They flickered, sending shadows dancing madly in the night. The stone basin beckoned, its silvery surface promising magic.

He placed thirteen floating white candles floated on the water's surface.

He lit the first one with a lighter, and then blew. The flame jumped from one candle to another until they all burned, tiny points of light under the crescent moon. He caught a glimpse of Daisy in the moonlight. While her eyes widened in surprise at the small bit of magic—a parlor trick, really—she didn't seem afraid. Merely...curious.

He slipped the lighter back into his pocket, then reached into the pouch tied at his side, pulled out a handful of acorns, and cast them into the water. He'd learned long ago that his magic was diluted, weak and unpredictable. The acorns helped to ground his magical energy—and they brought him a dose of good luck and a measure of protection.

"Stand at the other side of the basin," he instructed her.

He'd already committed to this. Best get it done and over with.

She stood there, hair tangled and wild, face scratched, her white peasant top stained with dirt. Bits of moss clung to her hair, and he fought the urge to reach over and pluck them out.

There was fire in her gaze, a steely determination. This was a woman who fought for the ones she loved.

Bitterness rose in his throat, but he swallowed it.

He'd long since learned it was a fool's errand to want things he couldn't have.

He waved his hand deosil—clockwise—over the basin.

"Gaze into the water and picture the mushrooms and where you found them," he instructed. The candles spun in a clockwise circle, the acorns bobbing like tiny autumn apples. Silvery magic wrapped around them like a glittering mist.

He hummed, a low, deep sound rising from his throat. Energy began to build, the mists glimmering and swirling around them.

"Danu, Mother of the Fae, we call on you. Bring to us what was lost. Bring to us what was lost. Bring to us what was lost." He repeated the phrase three times.

He held his hands over the basin. They'd sent out the call. Now all that was left to do was wait.

Nothing happened. Daisy looked crestfallen, and his heart lurched. Somehow, he didn't want to disappoint her. Somehow, he wanted her to see he wasn't just some grouchy recluse.

A buzzing sound reached his ear, like a swarm of bees drawing closer and closer. Leaving behind a trail of silvery light, the mushrooms, tucked safely into their basket, glided toward them.

Daisy's eyes widened. Knowing that magic was real was one thing; seeing it with your own two eyes was quite another.

The basket drifted into the courtyard and hovered above the basin. Daisy glanced at him. "You did that?"

He nodded. "Go ahead. Take the basket. It's yours."

He wanted to reach out and take the basket, deliver it gently to her waiting arms, but this was her battle, and he didn't want to interfere anymore.

Okay, to be honest, he wanted to share even the slightest of touches with her. His hands, brushing hers as he handed her the basket. His fingers, sweeping those wild chestnut locks away from her face, plucking stray leaves and bits of moss from those lavender-scented strands.

But he didn't have a right to do any of those things, so he held himself back.

Her hand shook ever-so-slightly as she reached out, taking it with trepidation. She inspected the contents of the basket and must've found what she was searching for because she held the basket to her chest. When she looked up, her eyes were wet. "Thank you, Rhett. But how did you—I mean, how does it work?"

"I don't ask questions. Magic has its own rules. I just follow them."

He exhaled deeply, grateful the spell had worked. It would be months until his weak magic recharged enough to do even a simple spell—not that he cared to.

The silvery mist began to dissipate as he released his hold on the magic.

And then he heard it. A haunting, high-pitched laugh that carried across the field.

A horde of fae of all shapes and sizes glided toward them. The changelings, with their bony bodies and too large eyes. The Fair Folk, tall and glistening. The dryad with her branches for hair.

They stopped at the low stone wall, and several of the changelings hissed. "You dare practice magic on our sacred night," the dryad said.

"I had no choice," was all he offered in reply.

He caught Daisy out of the corner of his eye. She clutched the basket like a life-preserver, but her back was straight. *Though she be little, she be fierce*, he thought.

One of the changelings leaned forward and pointed at him. "Death to the man and his tiny lady friend."

Rhett grabbed Daisy's hand and shoved her behind him, protective instincts kicking in. The changeling advanced. It cried out as it reached the iron-fortified wall.

The creature wore tattered brown clothes, covering skin that was greenish yellow and oddly smooth. And at its side glinted a dagger, sharp and lethal. It cried out an unholy scream as the iron touched its skin. It fell backwards, for the moment defeated. But Rhett wasn't taking any chances.

One of the Fair Folk, a man with brown hair streaked with gold, held out his hand.

Rhett's knees gave way as the blast of magic hit him. He gasped for breath that wouldn't come.

"Stop it!" Daisy screamed, and he heard her voice as if he were under water.

Remnants of his own magic still remained, silvery swirls of light lingering from the spell. He called them back to him. "Danu, protect me," he managed to gasp. "Protect. Her." He ground out the words. He couldn't allow Daisy to be harmed.

His own magic wrapped around them like an aura, repelling the faerie man's attack. Rhett gratefully sucked in a few deep breaths. The Fair Folk man's eyes narrowed, glinting at them in the dark.

"This isn't over," he said, eyeing the low stone wall as if debating whether it was worth it to try to cross it.

Rhett grabbed Daisy's elbow. "Hurry."

They fled toward the house, over lichen-speckled stone and tiny patches of grass. Past the gardenias and the roses they fled. He held fast to her elbow, not daring to let her go, fearing she'd slip once more into the fae's grasp and that this time, he wouldn't be able to rescue her.

He slammed the door and locked it. Relief flowed through him. He stared at her, at her pale blue glistening eyes, at the wild mane of hair framing her dainty face.

"Did they hurt you?"

She shook her head and clutched the basket. "No. But you. Rhett, are you okay?"

"Yes," he said, throat aching.

"You'll have to tell me how you did that thing with the basket. It was amazing. My experiences with magic have been rather...well, dark. But your magic is...wondrous." She smiled.

He raked a hand through his blond hair. "It's...I don't understand it myself. Ever since I was a boy, if I can picture something in my mind, I can call it to me. Nothing big. Not a person or a car. But a leaf, or a scarf, or a balloon. I just picture it, and it comes to me. Does that make sense?"

"I'm new to magic, but yeah, in its own way, it does."

He smiled, something inside him relaxing. He'd barely shared his magic with anyone, but he was glad he'd shared it with Daisy. Somehow, she understood, saw it as a source of wonder and not shame, and that somehow made it easier for him to accept it himself.

Daisy panted from the brief run—and from fear, no doubt. "What now?"

"My car is parked in the garage. We take it to your place and save your sister."

Those blue eyes pierced him. "Are you sure you still want to be involved in this? And what about them?" she said, jutting her chin toward the door.

"They'll go back to their revels and forget the likes of us. Hopefully they'll soon realize we mere mortals aren't worth their trouble."

He stepped forward, willing himself to release her. They were safely in the mansion now. The fae wouldn't dare come in.

"The garage is this way." He led her up the stairs, through the hall and kitchen and into the garage, flipping on the overhead light. He had three cars—a Land Rover, for when he wandered off the beaten path; a Lexus sedan, for everyday use; and a Corvette convertible when he needed the feel of freedom. The iron in the steel didn't bother him, with the magic in his blood being so little. But it would be enough to keep the faeries away from them until they could reach her sister.

He grabbed the keys to the sedan off the hook and climbed into the driver's seat. Daisy sat beside him, the basket in her lap as though she didn't want to let it go.

He caught the scent of lavender and clothes dried in sunshine and inhaled deeply. Something stirred deep in his belly, a feeling he hadn't allowed himself to feel in years.

Different. Daisy McAllister was different from anyone he'd ever met. She didn't seem to care about his money, and his magic seemed to intrigue her rather than frighten her. Perhaps she could deal with his fae lineage.

It didn't matter. Soon he'd deliver her to her home, she'd save her sister, and he would never see her again. He'd only known her a few short hours. Why should he care if he only ever saw her in passing at town fundraisers?

"Rhett?" she whispered as the garage door rumbled open.

"Yes?" His voice was hoarse and raw, his throat tight with a longing he tried to restrain.

"Are you okay? You just seem...I mean, I don't know you that well, but, did the fae hurt you back there?"

"No. Nothing like that."

I like you. Would that be so hard to say?

"Using magic drains me, that's all," he assured her. "I don't do it much for that reason."

She reached out and squeezed his knee, the familiar gesture taking him by surprise. "Thank you, then. For being willing to help a stranger."

He nodded, unsure what to say. She didn't feel like a stranger, and yet, for all intents and purposes, she was.

He turned on the car and started down the drive. She was a stranger. He was a man who liked keeping people that way—as stranger, at arm's length.

But when it came to Daisy McAllister, maybe he wanted more.

Chapter Four

T he old farmhouse she and her sister called home welcomed Daisy like an old friend.

It smelled of freshly baked bread and lavender. The living room was quiet, a braided rug over the worn hardwood floor, the brick fireplace still holding a few charred logs from the last chilly night a few weeks ago. The sofa and chairs were covered with layers of hand-stitched pillows, the coffee table a mess of books and receipts.

She sighed. *Home.*

Daisy turned to Rhett. Was he disappointed in the cluttered simplicity of the farmhouse?

If he was, he didn't show it.

"Lily's room is upstairs," she said. "Do you want to come with me to see if the magic works?"

It had better work. After all they'd risked...

"No." He shook his head. "This seems a family affair. I'll wait here."

She nodded. Somehow, knowing that Rhett was here made her feel more at ease. He said he doubted the fae would follow. But he hadn't said they couldn't follow. It wasn't just his magic or his knowledge of the fae that set her at ease, but his mere presence. Beneath the grumpy facade, she'd glimpsed a gentle soul and a kind heart.

Rhett settled into the sofa, sinking into the well-worn cushions. She watched him take up a Farmers' Almanac from the coffee table and begin to flip through.

Daisy made her way up the creaky steps, peeking into Lily's room. She seemed unchanged. In the third bedroom where they kept their crafting supplies, Daisy dug out the sewing kit.

Using needle and thread, she strung the mushrooms together.

She flicked on the light in Lily's room, heart pounding. The lamp was covered in a purple silk scarf, diffusing the light. It would probably be best. Lily's eyes hadn't fluttered open once these past two months.

Her bed had a cherry-stained headboard, and Daisy slipped the mushrooms over it and stroked Lily's hair.

"Come on," she whispered. "Work your magic."

She grabbed an old kitchen chair she kept nearby, one that they'd bought at an estate sale. She slid it over the rug and sat at Lily's side, waiting. How many nights had she sat here, reading *Little Women*—long a favorite of both of them—hoping that something she said got through to Lily?

She rubbed her hands along the chair's sky-blue painted arms. They'd spent a month's worth of weekends going to yard sales and estate sales, gathering a mismatched collection of kitchen chairs, and another Sunday afternoon painting them all the same shade of blue. Blue. Lily loved blue. Would her eyes ever spy it again?

Ten minutes passed. Then twenty.

The cuckoo clock's ticking seemed to haunt Daisy, each tick like the sound of a gong reverberating in her head.

Tick tock. *Two months*.

Tick tock. *Troll dust*.

Tick tock. *Wake up*.

Each flick of the second hand seemed to punch her in the chest. It wasn't working.

What would she do if it didn't work? She'd driven all the way to Savannah, where an elderly woman had amassed a collection of rare occult books. She'd been so kind when she'd heard of Lily's plight. When Daisy found the spell, she'd cried in relief, and the woman had been kind enough to allow her to simply take the book.

Everything was riding on this spell working, on those seemingly innocent mushrooms, charged with faerie power, drawing out the toxins.

Daisy searched her sister's face for signs the magic was taking effect. But her usually rosy cheeks were still pale as the moon. Her eyes flickered under closed lids, but that was usual.

As they approached the thirty-minute mark, Daisy's hope began to wane.

She went to the window and opened it, letting in the cool night air.

Somehow outside, an owl hooted. Crickets chirped. The creatures of the night, great and small, went on about their business.

Within the walls of their well-tended old farmhouse, Daisy's heart bounced between hope and despair a thousand times a minute.

She'd spent two months researching her sister's condition, and this was the only antidote she'd found.

"It has to work," she whispered to the night.

She heard the creak of the stairs and turned to find Rhett standing in the doorway. "Everything okay?" he asked, his voice low.

She gazed out the window, into the night's inky black, and sucked in a deep draught of fresh air. "Nothing is happening. I don't know what's wrong." Her voice squeaked.

She tried to will herself to be strong, but she'd been willing strength for two months, and she was starting to crack. Her hand went up to her mouth, and she stifled a sob. What if this was the beginning of the end?

"Oh, Daisy." Rhett rounded the bed and swept her into his arms. She leaned against him, letting herself sink into his embrace, letting go of the need to be the strong one for just an instance. "Give it time. Magic isn't always bippity, boppity, boo and then bam, it works. Sometimes it's slower than that. This might be slow magic."

"How slow?" she asked, leaning against his chest. "I mean, the troll dust took effect within a matter of seconds."

"That doesn't mean the cure will." He brushed her messy locks away from her face and cupped her cheeks, forcing her to look into his eyes. She saw warmth in them, and such kindness.

"I know it's naïve." She swallowed, forcing herself to voice her unspoken dream. "But I thought, come tomorrow morning, this would all be a nightmare from the past. I thought, Mom and Dad will come over, and we'll have a pancake breakfast, and everything will be okay. And now..."

"Come." He led her toward the blue chair at her sister's bedside. Lily slept on, oblivious to the world.

He sat in the chair and pulled her down so she was on his lap. In other circumstances, it would've been sexy, and her thoughts would've strayed somewhere indecent. But there was something sweet about the gesture, and she allowed his arms to loop around her, holding her, shielding her from what just might be a very ugly truth.

Fae magic had been powerful enough to push her sister into this wakeless sleep. Would it be enough to wake her?

The cuckoo clock sprang to life. First one chirp, then a second.

Two a.m. Lily had bought the clock during a semester abroad in Germany her junior year of college. She'd brought back all kinds of trinkets, none of them practical. A cuckoo clock. A collection of egg cups. Cookbooks written in German and collections of Grimm brothers' fairy tales—also in German, of course. Even though neither of them could say more than "danke schoen" and "auf wiedersehn."

"Oh, Lily." She slid off Rhett's lap, tears trickling down her cheeks. She held her sister's hand and leaned over Lily's still, unmoving body.

A moan cut through the night. It was quiet, barely a whisper, so soft Daisy wondered if she'd imagined it. "Lily?" She glanced at Rhett. "Did you..."

"I heard it too," he said.

She squeezed Lily's hand, brushed sleek brown locks away from her sister's face. "Lil? Can you hear me?"

Her sister stirred, a stretch moving from her neck and shoulders down to her toes. Daisy rose and swept the traces of tears off her cheeks, a smile finding its way to her lips.

Lily's eyes opened. Relief flooded Daisy, and she couldn't fight the stubborn but happy tears that followed.

Lily's eyes, that same shade of robin's egg blue Daisy had been longing to see, met hers. "What happened?"

"You...I...Trolls," was all she managed.

"I dreamt. Oh, Daisy," Lily said, squeezing her hand and fighting to rise to a sitting position. "I dreamed and I dreamed. Awful, terrible dreams. Dreams of dark fae, chasing me through the forest. It was...How long? Hours? Days?"

Daisy clamped a hand over her mouth and shook her head. Finally, she croaked, "Months."

"Months?" Lily's eyes widened. Color had been rising in her cheeks, the same pale pink that usually filled them, but she paled at the realization. "Months?"

"Two months." Suddenly, Daisy couldn't take it anymore. She lost all control, flinging her arms around her sister, losing the battle with her tears. "I missed you. I wasn't sure you were ever..."

Lily hugged her. "You saved me, didn't you?" She drew back, leaning into the stack of pillows and meeting Daisy's gaze.

"I did. With magic."

Lily traced a tear down Daisy's cheek, and Daisy smiled at the simple gesture. She'd never take her sister for granted again. She wouldn't complain the next time Lily made midnight brownies and didn't clean up the mess, or when she sang Spice Girls songs while harvesting herbs in the garden.

Thank you thank you thank you, her heart sang, to whatever deity would listen.

"Tell me how," Lily demanded.

Daisy perched on the edge of the bed and helped her sister rearrange her stack of pillows.

And then Daisy recounted her tale.

RHETT BACKED OUT OF the room, not wanting to intrude on the moment. He reminded himself he was a stranger here, just some man whose land happened to hold the cure to Lily's malady.

He was nothing to Daisy McAllister.

His chest stung with the idea of leaving. Maybe he would do his own shopping at the farmers' market from now on. Maybe he'd find a way to overcome prickly reputation.

Daisy made him want to be more. He wanted to be the man she seemed to believe he was. He wanted to be the man he'd been tonight—brave, self-sacrificing, unflinching, even when he had to use his magic.

That magic had seeped out of him now, flowed back into whatever parts of the earth it rose from, taking its silvery traces, its tongue that flicked his skin like the kiss of autumn mist, and vanished.

But it would be back.

He heard Daisy arguing—gently—with her sister. Apparently Lily wanted to shower—no wonder. She'd been asleep for two months—and Daisy thought it was unwise for her sister to be alone. Stubbornness must've run in the family, he thought with a smile.

Daisy. The thought of her name sent his heart racing. She made him want to be more. So how could he simply walk away?

"Fine. But you better not bash your head against the tile," came Daisy's muffled and exasperated voice through the half-closed bedroom door.

She slipped into the hallway and smiled at him, sheepishly.

"You stayed," she said, sounding surprised—but, thankfully, not disappointed.

"Yeah." He tucked his hands in his pockets, his eyes scouring the dimly lit corridor for anything to focus on. He settled on a small table that held a milk-glass vase full of gerbera daisies. "I wasn't sure—" he swallowed—"if you needed anything. But I can go." He started toward the stairs, finally certain he was intruding on some private family affair.

Daisy closed the small distance between them, rested her hand on his arm.

"Thank you for everything you did tonight. We're strangers and you..." She trailed off. Tears glistened in her royal blue eyes. But all that did was make them sparkle.

He heard the sound of drawers opening and closing in Lily's room, and Daisy sighed. With a nervous glance toward the door, she said, "Meet me downstairs. I'll be right down."

He made his way into a kitchen that smelled of freshly baked sourdough and the earthy scent of drying herbs. Her kitchen was a far cry from his. The appliances were old, and definitely not stainless steel. Drying herbs hung from the kitchen ceiling. There was a farmhouse sink and a well-used island with a butcher block top.

Life. That's what it was. This place bustled with it, with Daisy's warm energy.

He turned as she entered. She held out the tin. "Here."

He took it. "What's this for?"

"The burns on your hands. From the iron."

He inhaled sharply, his hands barely able to take the tin. She'd noticed. He waited for the other shoe to drop, waited for her to fill in the pause with words of rejection or judgment.

He stared down at her hands, her nails clipped short and unpainted. A few traces of dirt remained under Daisy's fingernails—whether from her skirmish with the fae, or from digging around in his woods, or from working her gardens here, he didn't know.

He swallowed. He only knew he liked it, and he wanted to see a lot more of those hands—a lot more of Daisy. There was a sweetness in her face, a down-to-earth warmth he'd never known before.

How had he seen her at that fundraiser and managed to walk away?

"Rhett?" she said his name, a mere whisper, like the rush of a gentle summer breeze.

He clutched the tin, its metal cool against his battered skin. "Yes?"

"I know."

"Know?" His throat was dry. He stared out the window above the farmhouse sink, into the inky black of night, afraid of what he'd see in her eyes.

"That you're part fae. That's why the iron burned your skin, isn't it? And that magic you used—it was fae magic, wasn't it?"

"Yes." The word stung his throat, a bitter truth he'd long ago learned to keep hidden. And while there were whisperings among some people in town, most were more interested in his money, in the scandalous end of his engagement, in his latest death-defying escapade in the Andes or Thailand. He wasn't too worried Daisy would tell anyone—those who believed must already suspect, and she'd risk the ridicule of those who didn't if she started going around telling people Rhett Fairshadow was a faerie.

He sighed. Part faerie. Mostly human, but with just enough of the fae in him to keep him outside the rest of the world.

He cleared his throat. "And now that you know..."

"And now that I know...nothing. It's just a part of who you are." He faced her then, the way he would face a mountainside he was about to climb.

"You mean..."

"I mean it's okay," she said, her voice soft.

Maybe she'd misunderstood. Maybe she was just caught up in the excitement of saving her sister. Any second now, she would realize what she was saying. Any second now, she'd realized she'd made a mistake. "But your sister...I mean, what the fae did to her."

"That wasn't you. You're a good man, Rhett Fairshadow." She stood on tiptoe and planted a kiss on his cheek. "Thank you for that."

A partial smile teased one side of his lips into a half-grin. And Rhett wasn't a man known for effusive displays of glee. His half-grin was a whole one.

But, if Daisy would have him, maybe that would change. He didn't know that he would be able to stop himself from smiling in her presence.

He glanced down at her and pushed her chestnut hair away from her face. He caught a whiff of lavender. "You truly don't care?" His heart thudded, a hammer against the wall of his ribs. He slipped the tin into his pocket as he waited for her answer.

"Not one bit," she said.

He leaned in, tilting her chin up and bringing his lips to hers. Her kiss—now that was magic, he thought as he explored her mouth. She tasted like strawberries, like sunshine and a summer's day. He cradled her face in his hands, and then slid his fingers through her tangle of chestnut waves.

Finally, they drew away, breathless.

This was the beginning of something.

He wrapped his arms around her, and she rested against his chest, and he was caught up in her spell, and he felt lighter and fuller at the same time.

It was a simple moment. Unable to resist, he kissed her again, deeper this time.

By the time the sun rose, everything had changed, his entire world taken apart, brick by brick, and rebuilt into more than he'd ever imagined possible.

The Faerie Key

Faerie Spells: Book 2

Chapter One

From the belly of the forest wild things called.

We were here before you, and we will be here after, the Fair Folk seemed to say.

Lily slipped out of bed. She wouldn't get any rest tonight. She didn't sleep many nights; she'd slept enough during those two months under the troll dust's spell.

Her sister, Daisy, dozed on in the room across the hall. Lily shivered despite the July night's warmth, reliving the nightmares that had tormented her, the twisted warren of haunting images that accompanied a troll-dust induced dream state.

She remembered running through a labyrinth of high boxwood hedges. The moon glowed overhead. Shadows writhed in the maze, reaching for her. Sometimes they would grab her, pull her down underground, and she would have to claw her way back out. She ran, but the shadows always caught her.

It had been a dream. She knew that. But for two months it had been her reality, her life. She didn't intend to go back.

Yeah. No wonder sleep eluded her.

Lily made herself a cup of sweet slumber tea, a blend of chamomile and valerian made from plants grown in the farm's gardens. But she knew it wouldn't help. Eventually, as the sun rose, she'd drift off into a world of fitful dreams, tossing and turning in a nightmare-filled slumber that was anything but sweet.

She turned off the gas stove just as the water came to a boil, not wanting the kettle's whistle to wake her sister.

Lily breathed in the floral scent of the tea and trod into the living room, where a plethora of books waited to occupy her insomniac mind. She'd been a night-owl before the incident. But this was different, a panic that filled her chest like a wild bird desperate to escape a cage.

Across the living room, on one of the shelves their father had made and gifted them, sat the collection of magical texts Daisy had amassed in her quest to cure Lily. Last time, Daisy had been there to rescue Lily. But soon, Daisy would leave, off to live with her fiancé. Already she spent less and less time at the farmhouse.

Lily had to do something to end this madness, this inability to step beyond the boundaries of the farm, this terror at closing her eyes. She had to find peace.

She ran her hands along the spines of the books, taking in the scent of the farmhouse, the smell of old books mixed with lavender and freshly baked pie. Maybe one of these books contained a way to break the panic's spell.

She wanted to be assured the fae would never upend her life again, but she knew there was no spell for that.

She tried to steady her racing heart. She would find a way.

What magic had done, surely it could undo.

THE NEXT NIGHT, LILY slipped out of the house, leaving behind the quiet laughter and companionship of Daisy and her fiancé, Rhett.

Silvery traces of moonlight shone down on the expansive gardens.

Lily loved the house she and her sister spent their spare time restoring, with all its quirks and character. But it was far too much a prison lately, surrounded by wilderness she dared not enter, surrounded by old oaks and maples whose serenity belied what lay in those woods.

Beyond the carefully tended rows of herbs—beyond the lavender, the rosemary, the thyme and the chamomile, beyond the orchards of apples and pears, the hedge of roses and lilacs—stretched the wild forests, teeming with fae.

Tonight, under the light of a July full moon, Lily would make sure that the fae couldn't come any closer. She couldn't drive them from these forests, but she could keep them from approaching the farmhouse.

Tonight, Lily McAllister took a stand.

But she didn't, wouldn't, couldn't tell Daisy and Rhett. They wouldn't understand.

Lily clutched the wooden box tighter to her chest. It was a deep red, the color of a dried rose petal, with a gold sun and silver moon on the top. It was a box meant for magic, and magic was precisely what she intended.

A gust of wind swept through the garden, carrying with it the scent of lavender and damp earth.

Beyond the moonlit garden, the forest lurked, full of mischievous faeries. They were quiet tonight, but she wouldn't be fooled. In those woods, the wild fae waited.

No more. Tonight it ended. Lily had found a spell in one of the tomes now housed in her living room.

Some of the books were new, their pages fresh and crisp and detailed with pen and ink drawings of flora and fungi used in magic and healing spells. Some were older than old, pages frail and brittle, filled with arcane language and long-forgotten magic-craft.

It was in a newer text, the cover bedecked with a cottage surrounded by rose bushes and hydrangeas, that she'd found this spell, one to protect the farmhouse and the six acres on which it sat from faerie magic.

She'd already placed the four stones that would create the circle of protection. One in the east, one in the north, one each in the west and south. Four chunks of black tourmaline, a powerful defensive stone.

Now, the spell. She withdrew a bundle of dried sage, a lighter, and a white pillar candle. She placed the candle on a large, flat stone where she sometimes sat and meditated, or simply contemplated life.

A shiver ran over her skin. She'd never attempted a spell before. What if something went awry?

A knot formed in the pit of her stomach.

What if next time something far worse crept out of those woods?

Sometimes at night, as she paced the house, she heard fey laughter pouring from the forest. They were getting closer and closer, bolder and bolder. How long before even the house was no longer safe?

And thus, the ritual.

Lily lit the candle, the flame flickering back and forth like a will-o-the-wisp. Hopefully its light would not lead her astray.

She lit the sage smudge stick, waiting until the dried leaves caught before blowing out the flame. Pungent, earthy smoke wafted into the air.

"Okay, Luna Hedgewood," she said, recalling the name of the author.

Spells for Hearth and Home, the cover had read. The inside was filled with pages edged with a leafy vine pattern and crammed full of spells and rituals.

"Don't steer me wrong," Lily said.

The sage smoke spiraled into the air. Lily waved the stick, and repeated the words she'd memorized.

"Protectors and wise guardians, I seek your aid. Protect house and home and those who dwell within. An it harm none, so mote it be."

A tingle went across her skin. The wind whipped up, sending her long brown locks billowing in the night air.

In the distance, thunder rumbled. Strange, because the night sky was clear as could be, the stars twinkling above, the moon's disc unobscured.

Lightning flashed.

Wait. Wasn't the lightning supposed to come first?

The wind began to swirl around her, whipped up into a frenzy.

Thunder cracked, directly overhead this time.

Oh, Lily. What have you done?

Light burst again, not from the sky but from the stone where the white candle burned. Hot and wild it shot through her. It didn't burn, surprisingly. Her body grew hot, like she had a sudden fever.

And then it was gone.

Her limbs grew weak and heavy.

"Lily!" She heard her sister's voice as though it were far away, much farther than the patio just across the yard.

The edges of the world blurred.

Rhett came running and caught her just as she collapsed.

"Are you crazy?" he demanded as he steadied her.

The world went in and out of focus. She perched on the edge of the rock, the candle's flame now extinguished by whatever magic had passed through it—and through her.

"Lily Evelyn McAllister, were you working magic?" Daisy demanded, hands on her hips. She may have been the younger sister, but she sure knew how to boss a girl.

Lily pressed her fingers to her temples. "A little protection spell," she managed. She looked up into Daisy's worried blue eyes. "What could it hurt?"

"What could it hurt?" Daisy repeated, her voice an octave too high. She swirled her hands in the air, as if that answered the rhetorical question.

Lily held her hands up. "I'm sorry. It won't happen again."

"No more magic," Daisy said, her voice dropping low. The wind had died down, leaving behind an eerie calm. "We've had enough to last a lifetime."

With that, her sister spun on her heel and walked through the back door and into the kitchen.

Rhett stood beside Lily, staring at the stone. "You shouldn't meddle with those forces, Lily. You of all people know that."

"I know. I just want us to be safe." Rhett's gaze traveled to the kitchen window. Through the screen door, Lily imagined she could hear the sound of Daisy stacking dishes in the sink—no doubt a little more roughly than was wise or necessary.

"I want that, too," he whispered, squeezing her shoulder. "Will you be okay?"

"I'm fine. Just a little dizzy."

He helped her inside. They sipped iced mint tea and ate rhubarb pie in uncomfortable silence.

The sound of night insects carried through the open windows. An occasional breeze tickled the lace curtains. All was calm in the wake of the spell.

In the light of the farmhouse, in the company of her sister and soon-to-be brother-in-law, she felt foolish. What had she been thinking? What good could come of magic?

She pictured the troll, its dark locks obscured by a ratty cap, heard its shriek as it launched the shimmering green dust at her face.

Lily stared out into the woods, fighting to steady her heartbeat. What if next time, they came for Daisy?

No. There wouldn't *be* a next time, Lily vowed.

Daisy looked up from the remnants of ice she'd been swirling in her glass. "We're going to head to Rhett's for the night. We're leaving for that trip to Asheville in the morning. Will you be okay for a few days?"

"Of course," Lily said, blushing. She knew how hard those two months had been for Daisy. She held up her hands. "No more magic. Just weeding the flower beds and packaging some tea mixes. Work stuff."

Daisy crinkled her nose. "And maybe a little fun. Just a smidge," she said, holding her thumb and index fingers apart a fraction of an inch.

"Just a smidge," Lily said, repeating the gesture, as she fought the urge to once more scan the darkened forest.

THE PAIN PIERCED HIS skull like an icepick. It was a pain he hadn't known for eleven years.

Neer had been chosen.

He dragged himself out of bed, letting the drab green quilt fall haphazardly onto the floor. He slept naked, and he fumbled in the dark for his clothes until he finally gave up and flipped on the flimsy bedside lamp.

Diffused light bounced off tan walls, accentuating the shadows that crept over the sparsely decorated, one-bedroom apartment he kept in the human world.

He hadn't been paired with a family in over a decade, not since that fateful night. Truth be told, he hadn't been ready then. He still wasn't now.

But the pain in his head that made the room seem to spin wouldn't stop until he reached his new family.

He grabbed a pair of black linen pants and an olive green shirt and tugged them on, not caring about his appearance. A connection spell could be undone, after all.

Maybe this family wouldn't want him. Especially after they learned what he'd allowed to happen.

Neer swallowed hard. He tried not to think about that night, about his failure, about the look in a mother's eyes as she saw Neer cradling her son's limp body in his arms.

He'd said no, no more, never again, and yet here was the pain.

"We are house-elves," his mentor had once said. "We don't choose where we're called or always know why. That is the way of our world."

Neer was a house-elf. Serving, protecting, guarding. These things ran in his blood sure as it ran red.

He grabbed a few things he'd need. He didn't know when, or if, he'd come back to this crappy apartment, but he'd learned to live with little. The walls were bare, the furniture all second-hand and well past its prime.

He slipped the golden key around his neck, feeling a slight static charge as the magic touched his skin. He owned nothing more sacred, nothing more powerful than that key.

The pain blurred his vision, and he braced himself against the wall. One more thing before he left this hovel. He slipped a knife holster onto his ankle and slid in a bronze dagger, its hilt in the shape of a roaring dragon, two rubies glittering like the creature's eyes.

He led a simple life. These things were all he needed.

Neer took a deep breath before he teleported, allowing the magic to guide him to his new charge.

Tonight, he would face his calling. For better or for worse.

TWO A.M. THE RED DIGITS on the alarm clock glared at her. Night after night, they mocked her.

With a sigh Lily rose, her bare feet meeting the cool hardwood floor. She grabbed a book off her nightstand and made her way downstairs. It was a second of Luna Hedgewood's books, *Spells for the Common Practitioner: A Beginner's Guide.*

Downstairs, the white sofa, piled high with floral patterned pillows in pastel hues, beckoned. The coffee table was scattered with natural living magazines, books on everything from organic gardening to vegetarian dining, and a few odds and ends.

She sat cross-legged on the sofa, a blue afghan draped across her legs.

Footsteps sounded on the front porch. A shiver ran up her spine.

Daisy had left hours ago and was no doubt asleep in her fiancé's arms, dreaming dreams of white dresses and four-tiered cakes. Had she forgotten something?

Lily checked her phone. No texts. Surely Daisy would've texted before she showed up in the middle of the night.

Lily sucked in a breath. The steps paused outside the door, and she heard a scrape of metal against the lock. At least she had locked the front door. Not that the rinky-dink lock would stop a determined burglar.

She tried to move, to run upstairs, to pick up her phone and call the cops, but fear froze her in place.

The lock began to glow, a golden light radiating from it, and it clicked open. Her heart lurched.

Rhett. She should've called Rhett. He knew how to handle unwanted fae visitors, even had a touch of magic.

But it was too late now. Startled into motion by the glowing lock, she leapt up and grabbed the nearest thing she could find: a blue, wheel-thrown vase she'd bought at a local art gallery. She hid behind the door.

It swung open. A man strode in—certainly not a human man, but a man nonetheless. She caught sight of muscled arms and shoulders clad in a green shirt, legs draped in loose linen pants. A fae man, she guessed by his magical means of entering.

She struck out with the vase, bashing the side of his head.

The vase cracked, but he didn't go down. He cried out and grabbed his head, spinning around.

"What was that for?" he yelled.

"For breaking into my house!" Her voice cracked, robbed of air. She shrank back against the wall, raising her now empty hands protectively.

"I didn't *break* in," he huffed.

He held up a gold key. The bottom looked like an ordinary skeleton key, but the top was an intricate design of spirals and knots with a green bit of peridot glistening in the center.

She backed toward the kitchen. Her keys were on the counter. She could run like hell out the back, hop in her car, pray the engine turned over, and make an escape.

"Okay," Lily said, her voice cracking. She wanted to run, but couldn't bring her legs to move. Bravado was the next best thing, right? "So you *magically* broke into my house."

"Why do you keep saying that?" he said. His voice sounded irritated—and confused.

Green eyes glittered in the lamplight, drawing her in despite herself. Black locks framed a handsome face—square jaw, aquiline nose, tanned skin. If only he weren't fae.

"You called me here," he said with an exasperated sigh.

"I don't know who you are," she said, fear fluttering like a sparrow's wings in her chest. She sucked in a deep breath. "But I didn't call you."

He stared down at her, as if unsure what to do with her. She took a few steps backward.

He glared. "You called." He pointed at her, as if she were an idiot. "I answered." He pointed back at himself.

"Like I said, I don't know who you are. So how could I call you?" Her words came out squeaky.

He seemed to catch himself. He rubbed his head where she'd struck him. Something wasn't right. He seemed...caught off guard, confused by her reaction. Did he think she wanted him here? In that instant, which of them was crazier?

"I'm Neer. Your house-elf."

Chapter Two

"My house-elf?" Lily almost laughed, but her throat was still tight with anxiety and it came out as a squeak.

This man, all six-foot-something of him, six-pack abs rippling under his too-tight shirt, was a house-elf?

"Aren't you supposed to be, you know, little?" Lily asked, holding her hand a few feet off the ground.

He sighed. "You're not a witch, are you?"

"No." She sucked in a deep breath.

"But magic was worked here recently," the man—Neer, he'd said in his gruff introduction—said with a sniff. "Someone summoned me."

She shifted her feet on the hardwood floor. "Oh. *That.* Yeah, I did that."

She watched him watching her, studying her, and something passed over her, but it wasn't the dread she'd expected.

She sighed, pushing such thoughts aside. She hadn't exactly known how the spell would work.

She recalled the shifting shadows of the tormenting dreamscape in which she'd lost two months of her life. The shadows, dragging her under, into the cold, dark earth. She couldn't let that happen again.

No, she'd had to do *something*.

But this...this wasn't what she'd intended.

"I cast a protection spell for me and my sister," Lily said. "But I didn't mean to call you."

"You asked for protection. Here I am." Something lurked beneath his words, a hint of bitterness like unsweetened chocolate or an unripe cherry.

She released a sigh of her own, some of the tension leaving her body. Not because he was here to protect her—she didn't need a bodyguard. But because he didn't seem to mean her any harm.

She forced the visions of the shadows away. She didn't know much about her late-night visitor, but she reminded herself that he probably wasn't here to sprinkle with her with troll dust. "Aren't you guys supposed to sweep the floors and make shoes?"

His green eyes were captivating, dark and unreadable, and a part of her relaxed, some knot of tension uncoiling itself. "You've read too many storybooks."

"Not possible." She started to pace, a nervous habit. "When I cast the spell, I just meant, you know, a magical force field around the farm. I didn't mean..." She waved her arm in his direction. "This."

"Magic has a mind of its own. You asked for protection. Clearly, the universe, that magical energy you're talking about, thought I was the solution."

Neer shifted, glancing around the farmhouse with a cautious gaze. He shoved his hands in his back pockets, rocked back on his heels and heaved yet another drawn-out sigh, as if this was the last place he wanted to be.

Was it because she didn't want him? Or because she wasn't a witch? Or something else entirely?

"Well, you can tell the universe I've changed my mind," Lily said.

She forced herself to stop pacing and crossed her arms over her chest. Clearly she'd wanted protection—that's why she cast the spell. But she didn't need some fae man skulking around the house—even if he did it with glittering green eyes, shaggy black hair, and an aura of mystery.

He raked a hand through his hair, casting his eyes toward the ceiling. "You called me. We're bound. If you want to break the binding, you have to wait until the new moon. Full moons are times for binding. New moons, for unbinding. Which you would know, if you were, in fact, a witch, not a mortal mucking with magic."

"I was trying to protect my sister," she murmured.

She pinched the bridge of her nose. This was one dream she wasn't waking up from.

"So what happens if you just waltz out of here like we never met?" Lily asked.

She sucked in a breath, her gaze traveling to the window. Why couldn't life go back to the way it used to be, simply two girls on a farm, tugging out weeds and plucking fresh chamomile?

True, nothing stays the same—Lily knew that much. But a life before the fae, a simple life. That was all Lily ever wanted. She'd gone to college, studied horticulture, dreamt of working the land, and now, at twenty-six, she was living that dream, thanks to a generous inheritance from a great-aunt named Marigold—Mari for short—that she barely remembered.

She'd had everything she wanted—for about half a second. And then the fae showed up.

And then she'd meddled with magic.

And now...now a brooding house-elf stood in her house. And by the looks of it, he didn't want to be there anymore than she wanted him there.

"For you, nothing would happen if I walked out that door," Neer explained. "For me? Unbelievable pain until you release me at the next new moon, or until I slip into a coma. Whichever comes first."

"Oh."

Lily didn't want him here, to be sure—didn't want a strange man in her house with her, didn't want to have to explain this little slip-up to Daisy when she got back from her trip.

Not to mention that he was fae, and she'd sworn off their kind.

But Lily couldn't be the reason someone was in agony and torment.

She watched him as he paced, obviously uncomfortable. His dark hair fell carelessly around his face, and she suspected it was the only careless thing about him. Once upon a time, she would've toyed with the idea of running her hands through those silky strands. She swallowed hard and looked away.

Because now...now she felt hollow, only half-alive. And even if he wasn't fae—which he was, she reminded herself—who would want someone who'd forgotten how to live?

He cleared his throat and rubbed his no doubt sore head. He glanced around the room. "Look. I don't want to be here;

you don't want me here. Why don't I do something useful? I could build a fire."

"It's July. The AC is on."

He paced back and forth in front of the fireplace so many times she wished he'd just build a fire and make the room ungodly hot.

"Do you want some iced tea?" she asked, her throat feeling parched. This was all too much.

"Would you like me to get you some?" he countered.

"No. I wasn't hinting. I was offering. Like you're a guest." She sighed and fought the urge to rub her temples. How long would it take to undo this mistake?

"But I'm not a guest," he countered.

The air simmered with July heat, despite the window unit blowing at full blast. Static electricity filled the room, making her hair stand on end.

"Damn it all," he muttered.

And then the lights went out, plunging the room into shadow.

She sucked in a breath and froze, fighting a wave of fear and cursing herself for being a grown woman afraid of the dark.

YINFIR, THAT SOULLESS bastard. It had to be.

Neer tried to get his bearings, but being bashed over the head with pottery didn't help.

Who was this woman, and why had the magic brought him to her door, of all places?

No. He had more pressing concerns. That shimmer of magic was all too familiar.

Yinfir, once a friend and now an enemy, had tracked Neer somehow. His house-elf magic was untraceable when not in use, but Yinfir had no doubt detected Neer's use of the key, for the first time in eleven years.

And now Neer's sworn enemy was about to make good on a decade-old promise: to end Neer's magic, once and for all—by taking his Ever Key.

The room grew unnaturally quiet. Not even the insects chirping outside, nor the hoots of owls, pierced the static-ridden silence.

There was a soft scuffing of leather-soled boots on the front porch. Neer tried to get between Lily and the intruder. Emotions rolled over him—loss, sorrow, regret.

He couldn't lose another one.

The lights flickered back on, though only at half power, their light dim in the night.

A figure stepped out of the shadows of the front porch and into the living room. Brown hair framed a face full of hard lines and sharp angles—high cheekbones, pointed jawline. Eyes pale as glacial ice, nose crooked from where Neer knew it had been broken in the man's youth.

"Yinfir," he said, backing up so Lily was behind him.

He hadn't been her house-elf for more than a few minutes and already she was in danger. Danger he'd brought with him. Why the fates had chosen him to guard her, he'd never know. So much of magic was a mystery.

Yinfir bowed. He wore a long, black leather duster that fell to his ankles—no doubt chosen to complete his look, to let the world know that Yinfir, formerly of the house-elves, was a bad ass through and through.

His lips pursed as he studied Neer. "Old friend. Long time, no see." Yinfir clenched fists and narrowed his icy eyes.

His gaze slid to Lily, who seemed confused, as though she couldn't decide whether to flee or stand her ground. "Yinfir of the house-elves, my lady," he said with a flourish.

"Stay away from her," Neer growled.

Yinfir feigned surprise. "I thought you would be more hospitable to your best friend."

Oh, they had been best friends once upon a time. In their youth, spending days climbing trees and practicing their tracking skills in the wild forests of home.

Their friendship had continued into the early days, when they'd each been assigned to a family. But that was before Yinfir allowed that ember of darkness inside of him to flare and consume him like a Beltane bonfire.

Yinfir always had a seed of darkness in him, a dark corner of his heart that the light couldn't reach. But once, Neer had believed in him. And that belief had cost him dearly.

After the death of his lover, Lenora, Yinfir had grown cold, distant, and the darkness began to grow. He blamed the family of witches she'd died protecting. Her death sent Yinfir on a path toward greed and shadow from which Neer couldn't bring his friend back.

The dagger. I should reach for it.

His hand twitched. In seconds he could draw the blade, end his former friend once and for all, save Lily and others.

But he couldn't. Because when he looked at Yinfir, he saw, beneath the darkness that now consumed him, the face of a beloved friend.

And that image, of a boy climbing a tree and urging a hesitant Neer to climb just a little higher, made him pause.

He tried to focus on the darkness. He knew Yinfir had long since left behind the role of protector, guardian, steward, and servant. It had culminated in Yinfir's betrayal, when he'd stabbed a knife into young Ignatius's chest and left him for dead, stripping the boy of his magic. Neer shivered at the memory of the green wisps of magic leaving Ignatius's body, filling Yinfir's chest as he drew the magic into his heart, his seat of power, letting the boy's power become a part of him.

Ignatius had been Neer's charge. And Neer had allowed him to die. Because he'd believed in his friend, tried to save him from his inner demons.

The house-elf council had taken Yinfir's Ever Key, a house-elf's most sacred gift. Neer's testimony about Ignatius's death had been the nail in the coffin, and once Yinfir's easy access to witches' magic had been taken away, he had sworn he would get Neer back.

So Neer had gone into exile. He'd thought Yinfir had moved on to greener pastures, but apparently not.

He might not be a house-elf anymore, but those years of stealing magic had made him a powerful foe. With every power he stole, every flicker of magic siphoned off a dead witch, Yinfir grew in power.

He already had the abilities of a house-elf—superior strength with which to defend their families, and the ability to teleport—but now he could do who-knew-what. Neer shuddered at what he was up against.

"Leave. Now," Neer said, his hand twitching at his side. "You can still choose a different path."

Yinfir's eyes traveled to Neer's hand, and something gleamed in those cold blue depths.

He raised his hand, curled his fingers and unfurled them to reveal a blue ball of electricity. His gaze was sharp, cutting. "You know better than that." The blue energy ball hovered above his hand, spinning, kinetic. "Give me the key. Let me finish what I started, or you will leave here once again a failure and a disgrace."

Neer's heart thudded. He pictured the life leaving Ignatius's eyes, his body going stiff and motionless. Neer stepped forward.

"Get. Out." The words came from behind him, full of threat—though even Neer detected the slight waver, the fear that laced those simple words.

"Lily, no," he said, trying to shield her as she stepped around him.

Yinfir unleashed the flickering orb. It bounced off the wall, shattering a mirror framed with driftwood and sending a pair of sconces crashing down. Neer grabbed Lily and pushed her to the floor, shielding her with his body.

The ball ricocheted off the wall and clipped him in the shoulder. Shards of pain lanced his shoulder and arm. He fell on top of Lily with a thud. The key fell out of his hand and landed on the blue braided rug that cushioned the hardwood floor.

Yinfir leaned over him. "You always were such a good boy. Even as a child, rescuing injured sparrows. But I don't care about the woman. Though whatever magic she possesses is...peculiar. No. This time, I want the key." His eyes glinted in the dim light.

Neer reached out for the key, but pain shot down his arm, paralyzing him. Yinfir stepped on Neer's outreached hand, and he cried out, a thousand curses thundering like wild horses in his brain.

Yinfir grabbed the key.

"Good night, old friend." He stormed out the door.

The lights flickered and went out again, plunging Neer and his new charge into the black.

He rolled off Lily and leaned back against the couch, clutching his injured arm.

"Hold on," she said.

He heard the sound of her rummaging through a drawer. She flipped on a flashlight and came to his side, kneeling in front of him and shining the beam on his shoulder.

Brown hair framed her face, and he caught the scent of coconut shampoo and something that smelled like strawberries. That lip balm stuff that human women loved so much, perhaps?

She was by far the most beautiful of all his charges. Sleek brown locks now slightly disheveled from the scuffle, robin's egg blue eyes with concern swimming in those deep pools. He sighed and shifted, leaning back into the couch.

"I don't see any blood," she said. "That must be a good sign."

"The pain will pass," he assured her, stretching, trying to catch his breath. "We have bigger problems."

She touched his arm, her hand cool against his burnt skin. A part of him ached for such a caress, for those slender fingers pressed against his chest.

He shook his head, clearing his thoughts. He couldn't afford to get entangled with this woman. He'd cared deeply for his last family, and look where that had gotten him.

"You mean the key he took?" she asked.

"It's not just any key," Neer said.

"I gathered that much."

"You don't understand." Neer tried bringing some movement into his shoulder as he spoke, gritting his teeth against the pain. "It's an Ever Key."

"A what now?"

The lights flickered back to life, revealing the genuine confusion—and concern—in those impossibly blue eyes.

No. He was *not* going to think about her eyes. And he was definitely not going to imagine himself getting lost in them.

"Every house-elf is entrusted with a master key," Neer said, the explanation a convenient distraction. "It can unlock any door, even one sealed by magic. It can break through magical barriers."

"And why does this guy want this magical key?" she asked, arms crossed over her chest. She was a strange mixture of defiance and kindness, fear and courage, wit and naivety. At least, naivety when it came to magical matters.

"He wants what it can bring him. Power. Lots and lots of magical power. With the key, he can enter the house of any witch he wants, and steal their magic."

A shadow crept over her features. She gazed at the still open front door, as if steeling herself.

"So," she said, her voice a hoarse whisper. "What happens now?"

Chapter Three

B lood thundered in Lily's ears. She'd cast the spell to keep the fae out of her life, and now they were pouring in. Meddling with magic had been a colossal mistake.

She sighed. "Has he, already, you know, *poofed* his way out of here?"

Neer smiled, a crooked smile that somehow set her a little more at ease. "Poofed?" He raised an eyebrow.

"Well, that's how you both got here, isn't it?"

"Ah, yes. Teleportation, as you humans would say. No. I think he's nearby. That energy ball he sent our way would've temporarily drained his powers. No doubt the spineless rat is cowering in the woods somewhere."

She worried her lower lip, willing her heart to stop racing. She focused on the room, on the stack of magazines on the table, on the conch shell, chunk of amethyst, and framed photos on the fireplace mantel. All that was safe and familiar. Anything but the forest.

Is this going to be your life, Lily McAllister? Cowering in this farmhouse like you're Rapunzel locked away in a tower?

No. She'd made this mess. If not for her, Neer would be sleeping in his bed, his key safely around his neck—or wherever the heck he kept it. Her misuse of magic had called him here and set tonight's events in motion.

So, paralyzing fear or not, she had to help him. That was who she was. Not some whimpering ninny.

"First, we have to see to that wound," she said. "Wait here."

She fled quickly up the stairs, to the tiny third bedroom she and Daisy used to store inventory and various projects. She rummaged through a plastic drawer until she found a tin of homemade herbal salve, grabbed the first-aid kit from under the bathroom sink, and made her way back downstairs.

Neer sat on the sofa, eyes green as emeralds, staring out past the lacy curtains into the inky night beyond. He seemed far away, and part of her wanted to draw him closer, to pry those secrets from his shrouded heart.

Which was crazy. Because, seriously, she didn't know the man.

She shook her head, the last stair creaking under her weight, and he turned toward her, and his expression was all grim business again.

"What's this?" he asked.

"Before you go traipsing through the forest, that wound needs to be cleaned."

He sighed and moved in his shoulder in a half-circle, then abruptly stopped. "I've had worse."

"Maybe." She sat beside him on the sofa and prayed he didn't notice the ever-present tremble in her hands.

It wasn't always like this...

"Take off your shirt," she said.

He grinned, crookedly, a sight so unexpected that it was infectious, and the corners of her mouth twitched in response. "So I can clean your wound," she added hastily, her throat dry.

Those green eyes twinkled. She almost forgot that the only reason he was here was that she'd made a magical mess of epic proportions. Almost.

"You didn't have to do that, you know. Take the magical equivalent of a bullet for me," she said.

"It's who I am." The words were simple, plain, without an ounce of pride in them. He wasn't bragging. He was stating a fact.

She tried to let that sink in.

Because he was a house-elf, or because of the kind of man he was?

Or, perhaps, both?

He tugged off his olive green shirt, and she tried not to stare at his bare chest. The wound was raw and pink.

"Neer?" she nearly whispered, sucking in a deep breath.

"Yes?" he said, his voice sounding a bit rough.

"I'm not going to lie. This is going to hurt like a mother."

"Like a mother?" That grin again, as though her strange human ways were infinitely amusing.

But this time she couldn't smile back, just stare, just itch to touch his skin.

What was wrong with her?

Soon enough she'd send him packing. Nothing personal. Just that she didn't need some fae bodyguard looming over her night and day, wearing a path in the living room floor, staring pensively out into the night.

She pressed an antiseptic wipe against the wound, and he flinched, then remained remarkably—some might say stoically—still.

How dangerous a job was being a house-elf, that his pain tolerance was that high? She shivered to think what nightmares this man had seen.

She opened the tin of salve, the scent of aloe vera, rosewater, and coconut oil soothing her senses. His fingers pressed into the white slip-covered couch, almost imperceptibly, as he braced for her touch.

"This is a nasty burn. It will hurt at first, but I promise the salve will help." She tried a soft smile and held up the tin. "Patent pending."

Her joke only seemed to perplex him. And why wouldn't it? They were literally from different worlds.

She swiped her fingers through the salve and pressed them lightly against his skin, feeling only the slightest of flinches under her touch as she rubbed a small circle into the grapefruit-sized wound. His skin felt feverish under her fingers—perhaps a side effect of taking an...energy ball...to the shoulder.

And if her touch lingered half a second too long, if she forgot she was tending his wound for half an instant, hopefully this strange, brooding man would forgive her.

With a sigh she ripped open the gauze and pressed it over the disinfected wound.

"Almost finished?" he asked. He gaze on her was...intense. A man like that could keep a girl spellbound. Was that his magic, or had Lily just been holed up in the farmhouse too long?

She fished out the surgical tape and ripped off a piece. "Just about."

He waited in what she could only call pensive silence.

Tending his wound, lost in a strange sea of emotions, an odd combination of attraction and guilt and worry, she could almost forget that there was one more dark fae than usual in the forest.

The thought slammed into her like a freight train. The forest. The fae.

"All done. Hold on and I'll get you a clean shirt. Yours is a little...charred."

She headed upstairs to find one of the spare shirts Rhett kept around the house for impromptu sleepovers. When she returned, a plain black tee in hand, Neer had taken up pacing again.

"I need a way to track him," he said.

Ah. So the spell of attraction she'd sensed? Definitely one way. She was tingling in all the wrong—or perhaps, right—places, and he was already moving on to the next thing.

"A magical way to track him?" she asked, handing him the shirt.

He slipped into it, seeming a million miles away.

"Mmhmm," he responded, absently.

He stopped in front of the fireplace, ran his hands along the oaken mantel, traced the mortar in between the bricks. His dark hair fell across his face. She sucked in a breath.

She plopped down on the sofa, sinking deep in the cushions.

A shiver slithered up her spine despite the humid night. Too much. It was all too much.

No, instead she would focus. One problem at a time, as Daisy would say.

So, Lily took a deep breath and tried to concentrate on the issue at hand. *Mess. You made a mess.*

"What about scrying?" she finally blurted out.

He paused, turned to her. "That could work. Do you have the implements? A pendulum, a local map?"

She smiled, ignoring the lump in her throat. "I have a quartz pendulum I bought years ago. I could never get the thing to work, but maybe you can, you know, use your faerie magic."

He cocked his head, nodded. "Yes. But what about a map of the area?"

"I think I can help with that, too."

She made her way upstairs and into the spare bedroom again. She dug around in the drawers of a dresser until she found the pendulum, a pointed piece of clear quartz dangling from a silver chain. She grabbed the map from the wall—frame and all—and carried the two downstairs.

"The kitchen will work best," she said as she reached the bottom of the stairs.

She led him into the kitchen. The earthy scent of drying herbs washed over her, soothing her. This was where she and Daisy made the teas they sold at the local farmers' market, and those many hours working side by side made the kitchen a place of comfort, a place where she could relax and forget about her woes.

A large oak table surrounded by mismatched chairs await-ed them. She moved the bins of packaged teas, the blue teapot with its matching cups, and a blue pottery bowl and set the map on the table.

She dangled the pendulum in front of him. "Do you know how this thing works? Because I tried to use it once, and I ended up on the expressway to Nowheresville."

He smiled, studying her. His nose was slightly crooked, his cheekbones high. He was undeniably handsome—even more so when he wasn't scowling. "Nowheresville?"

"You know what I mean." Okay, maybe he didn't. "It didn't work."

She clutched the pendulum, willing her hands not to tremble. They always trembled these days.

She circled the pendulum in her hand. As a girl, she'd longed to have magic in her blood. But she couldn't work a pendulum, and her protection spell had gone admittedly wrong. Now, instead of keeping the fae away, it seemed to have made the farmhouse a magnet for fae men.

Neer took the pendulum from her hand and studied the map. "This map is wonderfully detailed," he said as he leaned over it. "Where did you get it?"

She gazed down at the map. "My father. Cartography is one of his hobbies. He gave it to me and Daisy as a housewarming present when we inherited this place. It's the farmhouse and surrounding areas."

Hand-drawn on ivory paper, the map showed every landmark within a five-mile radius. Every farm, every barn, each pasture, every abandoned building. The stream that bordered their land and coursed through the woods. The farmhouse was in the center of the map, the surrounding forests and farms radiating out from there.

Neer clutched the pendulum in his hand, his brow creased in concentration. He pulled out one of the pale blue chairs that surrounded the table and sat. Shadows fell across his face, highlighting his rugged features.

Lily fought the urge to run her fingers through those sleek, dark locks as they framed his face. She fought the part of her that was drawn to him like a moth to a flame.

Come the new moon, this man would be out of her life. She'd find another means to keep the fae at bay.

He sat and leaned over the map, dangling the pendulum. It swung with the movement of his hand, but then it stilled. He closed his eyes and leaned his head forward, a reverent expression on his face.

The pendulum stilled. Lily clutched the back of one of the chairs and held her breath, waiting.

A silvery wisp of light radiated from his hand, spiraling around the pendulum, traveling down the silver chain to circle the polished clear quartz.

The light disappeared, and the pendulum began to swing and sway. Slowly, as though an unseen force tugged on the chain, it pointed in one direction, pulling Neer's hand and the pendulum away from the farmhouse and deep into the woods.

Neer opened his eyes and stared down at the map. With his free hand, he pointed. "What's this?"

"An abandoned house. Kinda creepy." Okay, really creepy, if she were being honest.

"That's where he is." He tapped the glass that covered the map. Something dark skittered across his features, his scowl returning. She didn't like that look.

"What is it?"

His eyes met hers, a grim expression tinting those dark green pools. "I can't shake the feeling that we're walking into a trap. Yinfir has the advantage."

Her gaze traveled to the back door, picturing the gardens and hedge and the forest beyond.

"Can we call for backup?"

Surely he had fae friends who could help—much as she shuddered at the thought of bringing even more faeries into her life.

He shook his head. "Backup?" Her turn of phrase seemed to amuse him, but then the darkness returned. "By then, it will be too late. No, we must go now and face whatever Yinfir has in store for us."

She clenched her fists, eyeing the door. The last time she'd ventured into the woods at night, she'd lost two months of her life. And this time they knew there was a faerie awaiting them, intent on doing them harm.

"Are you so sure it has to be a *we*?"

Lily was wavering now, torn between fixing the damage she'd caused and a relentless fear that chased her like an angry hornet.

"Afraid so. Until the bond is solidified, I can't be more than a few yards away from you. And that could take until sunrise. Is that a problem?"

"I just...thought you were supposed to, you know, protect. How is dragging me into a forest full of fae protecting?" In the same breath she cursed herself. This was *her* mess.

But as soon as she thought of entering the wood, she imagined those shadows, dragging her down under the earth. She could never explain to anyone how much that frightened her.

Warring emotions threatened to tear her in two.

On the one hand, responsibility to clean up a mess she'd caused.

On the other, the feeling of clawing her way back out of the dark, loamy earth, her fingers scratched and bleeding. Nothing had ever felt so real.

Not again. Not a panic attack, she told her increasingly shallow breaths. Not now. *You cannot fall apart now.*

"It's one of the flaws in the magic. It's meant to keep us together, help us bond. But it doesn't account for every situation." He ran his fingers through his shoulder-length black hair. "Such as this one."

"But aren't you, you know, a house-elf? Shouldn't you protect the house?" She waved her arm, gesturing toward the room, willing her breaths to deepen.

"House-elves attach themselves to people or families, not to homes. Otherwise, if you moved, I'd be left behind. Make sense?"

"As much as anything else you've told me," she muttered.

"What, are you afraid of the dark?" He quirked an eyebrow in an arrogant expression that irked her.

"No..." Well, she was, wasn't she? "If you must know, something happened to me in those woods. Something involving the fae. I'm just not too keen on going back."

He nodded, his expression softening. "And let me guess. That's why I'm here?"

She swallowed. "Something like that."

He tapped his fingers on the glass atop the framed map, studying her with his head cocked. "I'm sorry. I wish there were another way. But there are..."

"Other lives at stake? I know." She sighed.

She thought of what he'd told her, of the witches who would be murdered in their beds if Yinfir escaped with the key. She couldn't have that on her conscience.

But she also couldn't face those woods.

Lily crossed the kitchen and stared out the window over the farmhouse sink.

"I don't know if I can. You don't know what's happened to me in those woods, at the hands of the fae."

A solitary tear dripped down her cheek, tracing a salty path down her skin. Daisy had risked her life to save Lily from the troll dust's spell, from the slumber and the nightmares from which there had seemed no escape. Lily didn't want her sister's sacrifice to be for nothing.

Neer came to her side and rested his hand on her arm. "I don't pretend to know what you've faced, but I am your house-elf. I will protect you."

She wiped the tear away, willing away any others that wished to follow. There was a reason she'd cast that protection spell. She'd wanted to protect herself and her sister. She couldn't bear the idea of being helpless, at the mercy of the fae.

No. If she went into those woods, it would be with her head held high. She wouldn't cower.

Lily nodded and steeled herself. She was still terrified, but she had to push through. For Neer. For those Yinfir might harm if he was allowed to keep the Ever Key.

"Okay. Let's go into the woods."

Chapter Four

N ight and its shadows surrounded them.

Lily's heart thundered in her chest like a solo at a drum circle—one played by a rather obnoxious drummer who didn't know when to yield his time. She sucked in shallow breaths as they crossed the yard and its sprawling gardens.

The gardens were the main reason she couldn't simply sell this place, however fae-infested the surrounding forests might be.

She and Daisy poured their heart and soul—not to mention a great deal of their savings—into those gardens. To leave would be to give up the business they'd inherited and grown from their aunt's quirky enterprise designed to supplement her retirement checks to a bustling business that paid the bills.

Lily and Neer passed a row of rosebushes, heavy with summer blooms. The trees loomed ahead of them, oak and ash and maple guarding the secrets of the fae.

Neer held a glowing white orb in his hand. She clutched a flashlight in hers.

Her pulse thrummed. She felt an unseen link, subtly pulling her toward him, and she resisted the urge to reach out to him, to seek solace in a stranger's embrace.

It had to be the magic, she told herself.

Lily stopped at the edge of the wood. They walked the same path she and Daisy had taken that fateful night.

Lily had changed out of her running shorts and tank top and into a pair of jeans and a gauzy black top with spaghetti straps. She'd tucked a few magical implements into her pocket: a hunk of raw, unpolished quartz and a piece of shining bloodstone for protection.

She'd donned a hematite ring, the shimmering stone cold against her skin. Hematite reminded her of her own power, and now more than ever, she needed that reminder.

Not that she wanted to use anymore magic. But who knew what they were walking into. A girl had to be prepared.

Her feet were clad in a pair of teal sneakers. Perfect garb for running from the fae. Except she wasn't running from them. She was running toward them.

You had to go and meddle with magic. You silly, silly girl.

Neer studied her in the darkness. He reached out and brushed his fingers over her bare arm, and she shivered—not a shiver of fear, but one of excitement at his touch.

"Are you ready?" he asked, his voice like a velvety caress.

She shook her head. "I don't know that I'll ever be ready."

But she'd be damned if she was going to keep cowering in the farmhouse for the rest of her life. No, panic-inducing or not, she was going into those woods. She'd made this mess, and she would clean it up.

She put one foot in front of the other and entered the shade of those towering trees.

The forest smelled of pine and ferns, damp earth, fresh leaves. It should've comforted her. Once upon a time, the forest had been a peaceful place, a refuge where she could daydream and wander aimlessly.

But that had all changed after the troll attack. She hadn't entered the forest since—not even in broad daylight, let alone at night when the fae roamed the forest's paths.

But Neer said the key was important, and really, what did he have to gain by lying to her? He had risked his life to save her from that flying orb of death—or whatever it had been.

"How's your shoulder?" she asked, her voice quiet, but still piercing the sleepy forest.

Anything to take her mind off what she was doing, off the trembling of her limbs, off the dread that surged in her with each step she took deeper and deeper into the wood.

"Been better," he grunted.

"You and Yinfir have a history," she said, desperate for distraction.

"Believe it or not, once upon a time, we were best friends."

"But he went to the dark side, and now he's after your Ever Key." The words felt strange on her tongue. But magic was a part of her life now—it had been, whether she'd realized it or not, since the moment she and Daisy set foot in Foster Springs.

"Long story short, yes," Neer said. He offered no more details about what had to be some serious history between him and Yinfir.

They walked in silence. She clutched the flashlight, the beam of light doing little to keep the inky shadows at bay. The forest was quiet except for the occasional hoot of an owl.

Neer held the glowing sphere in his hand. It was tiny, the size of a baseball, but it put out a fair amount of light.

He knelt, tracing his fingers along the ground, on the soft outline of a footprint that remained in the soil.

After a moment, he nodded. "Yes, he passed this way."

He studied the earth intently, and then rose, brushing dirt off his knees, and continued toward the abandoned house where who knew what fate awaited them.

Wind rustled the leaves in the towering trees. She heard roosting birds settling in the high branches. The full moon pierced the canopy, a watchful eye in their travels. Lily's breath came a little faster than necessary.

Neer turned back to her. "Are you unwell?"

She nodded. "I just...I used to like moonlit strolls, but now..."

He squeezed her shoulder. "I am your house-elf. I will protect you."

She didn't know him very well, but she believed him. "Why?"

"It is my duty."

His duty. She couldn't imagine living the rest of her life with a personal bodyguard. She'd cast a spell for protection, sure. But was this really what she wanted?

No. What she wanted was to be strong. Perhaps what she really wanted wasn't protection, after all, but courage.

And Neer seemed to have his fair share. Perhaps that was why the magic had brought him to her? Not to protect, but to teach.

That was it then. She would learn something from him, and then she would set him free. Because he seemed like a good man—concerned for others, dedicated to his duties—and he deserved to be free.

Come the new moon, she'd release Neer from his bond to her, and he could be free to serve some other family. And then she would find some way to stay safe in a world of fae.

Fighting to steady her racing heart, she followed Neer and his silent footsteps deeper into the forest.

NEER HELD UP HIS HAND in a "stop" gesture.

They were close. His magic told him, nerve-endings tingling with currents of magic.

He held his head high, sniffing the air. That scent could only mean one thing. "I smell fae magic—dark fae magic."

"And what does magic smell like?" Lily asked, though he couldn't tell whether she was curious or merely trying to distract herself from her fear.

He raised an eyebrow. He'd forgotten that non-magic humans couldn't detect the aroma of magic, let alone distinguish the different types.

Although hadn't Yinfir said...did Lily have magic? But she wasn't a witch.

No. If Lily did possess some latent magical ability, that was a mystery for another time.

"Depends on the type of magic," he said, returning to her question. "Your protection spell smelled like cloves and fresh cut grass. Yinfir's magic is darker, smells like...myrrh."

The scent grew stronger the further they crept. Neer paused and withdrew his dagger, the blade glinting deadly in the moonlight.

Their path took them deeper into the heart of the forest. They walked along an old creek bed, long since dry, pocked with rocks and piled high with fallen leaves. The earth was squishy beneath his feet.

They climbed out of the creek bed, his innate magic following the traces of magic Yinfir had left behind.

Neer offered Lily his hand. Her touch sent a heat coursing through him that had nothing to do with the magical link between house-elf and charge.

He wouldn't lie; he liked her. Clearly the wood set her on edge. But here she was. Beyond her fear, beyond whatever the fae had done to her, she had a fire in her spirit.

He didn't release her hand right away, even as she stood next to him on the embankment. Her skin was warm. The scent of strawberries and coconut washed over him again, drawing him in.

He met her vibrant blue eyes, and, without thinking, he brushed the wild brown locks away from her face. He brushed his knuckles against her flushed cheek, gazing into those eyes.

She leaned into his touch, and for a moment, he let himself forget everything else.

He caught himself and drew back, turning away. She must hate the fae, after what she'd been through. And she'd made it clear that she didn't want a house-elf.

They would be, as someone once said, like two ships passing in the night. Their link would be brief.

But oh, what a fire it could be.

She was different than the fae women he knew from home; her features were softer, gentler. She had this energy that he admired. And she was beautiful. Brown locks surrounded a sweet, freckled face and a pair of gorgeous eyes the color of robin's eggs. And she'd had the moxie to clobber him with a vase.

Yeah, if he had to serve and protect anyone, he was glad it was Lily McAllister.

A wave of discomfort swept through him. He'd guarded three families in his time as a house-elf, and he'd never felt this sort of attraction to any other human he'd protected.

He clenched his fists. He'd led her into danger, seeking out Yinfir and the Ever Key. Some house-elf he was.

He saw the darkened outline of a house up ahead. Its white siding was peeling and lichen-covered in the fae-light's golden glow. Plywood covered the windows, and someone had spray-painted a red anarchy symbol on the side. The front porch of the small house sagged. Someone had broken in the front door.

Is this what you've reduced yourself to, Yinfir? Hiding in falling-down houses in the middle of the wood?

There was no use hiding their approach. Yinfir knew Neer's tracking skills were unrivaled, and surely he also knew that Neer wouldn't give up his Ever Key without a fight.

Neer remembered a different wood, long ago, when he and Yinfir were twelve or thirteen, still living in the forests of the Elven Realm, honing their tracking skills at the academy, biding their time until they were called to serve a family and given their Ever Keys.

The trees had grown ancient and tall, lichen-speckled, moss dangling from their twisting branches. The whole world seemed hushed as he and Yinfir watched the doe and her two fawns drink from a clear pool. She lifted his head as if she sensed them.

Neer raised his bow, but he couldn't let his arrow fly. The image of that arrow digging into the doe's chest, stopping her heart, was too much for Neer.

Yinfir hadn't had the same sense of wonder, the same awe at the mother and her spotted younglings. He did not stop to ponder. *What would happen to the fawns if their mother was taken away?*

Yinfir didn't hesitate. He let his arrow fly. The doe stumbled and fell. "Tonight we feast on venison," he'd cheered.

The fawns had taken off into the woods, crashing through the underbrush, and Neer had turned away so his friend wouldn't see the solitary tear that trickled down his cheek.

What had they done?

Lily approached the house, but Neer grabbed her arm. Pain shot through him. He'd almost blocked out the blinding, searing ache that he felt in his left arm every time he moved it. Almost.

He was torn. He couldn't leave her out here alone. Yinfir might come after her. But inside the house certainly lay a trap.

There was no choice, though. They'd both have to go in together. "Let me go first," he said.

The wooden porch seemed to sag under his weight. The situation was almost certainly a trap. But what choice did he have? Soon Yinfir's magic would be recharged, and Neer would have no chance of retrieving the key. He had to act now.

The front door stood partially askew, and he gently pushed it open. The old, rusty hinges creaked in protest. He tested the floor inside. Weak, but strong enough to hold his weight. Not rotted through, at least.

He took a few steps into the small living room. The place was empty save for a battered table and a couple chairs, all toppled on their sides. Curtains, perhaps once rosy pink, were now stained and darkened. It was a far cry from Lily's rambling farmhouse, packed full of charm and earthy décor.

He gestured to her to follow. Eerie silence filled the house, broken only by the sound of squeaking floorboards and the scuff of his leather boots against the wood. He clutched his bronze dagger in his hand, holding his breath, waiting for Yinfir to strike.

Neer paused. A strange, unwelcome scent tickled his nose, something out of place in the old house.

Lilacs.

Which could mean only one thing. A piskie was near. They weren't malicious creatures, but they were mischievous, and could be easily persuaded to wreak havoc.

The creature in question shot out from behind the curtains. Like a large hummingbird, she zoomed past him, sparkling with silvery magic.

Neer jumped back, lost his focus, and the fae-light snuffed out.

Only the beam of Lily's flashlight broke the darkness that followed.

He managed to get the fae-light going again, refocusing his magic on powering the light. It didn't take all of his concentration, but just enough. The light sprang back to life.

The piskie hovered before him, willowy and tiny, not more than ten inches from the top of her head to her dainty toes. She wore a ragged tan and mossy green dress.

Her large eyes stared at him. She clutched a large bag in her hands, holding it by the strings. She flew toward the ceiling and the bag hovered in mid-air.

The pouch tilted, its contents falling to the ground. The piskie waved her tiny hands, and the contents spilled and began to form a circle.

He realized, too late, what he was up against: iron oxide. The red dust encircled him, binding his magic and trapping him. What was worse was that Lily was on the other side of the circle, separated from him by the foul dust.

"Lily. Run!"

There was no other option. He couldn't protect her now. Blinding pain or not, he needed her to run.

"I'm not leaving you," she said, blue eyes flashing. She glanced at the dust, no doubt quickly assessing the situation: iron circle equals fae prison. "How do I free you?"

"You don't," a haughty voice said.

Yinfir practically glided in, stepping through a doorway that led to some other part of the house—the kitchen, most likely. His leather boots scuffed gently against the dirt and grime covered hardwood floor.

Neer stood frozen. Anytime he got too near the circle that surrounded him, a tingle erupted all over his skin. Any closer and his skin would start to burn.

Yinfir approached Lily. "He shouldn't have brought you, but I knew he would. Silly house-elf rules. I'm glad I extricated myself long ago."

Yinfir moved quickly as a cat pouncing on a mouse and struck her so hard she hit the floor.

She rose partway, but he pressed his boot-clad foot against her back and pinned her down. She cursed at him and struggled, not going down without a fight. She might've feared the forest and the fae—and with good reason—but she was no coward.

Yinfir dragged her, kicking and screaming, to one of the chairs, and tied her up.

Neer flung himself at the circle, like a wild bird suddenly stuffed into a cage. He roared when it burned his skin, stepping back and doubling over, arms crossed over his chest.

He recalled the helplessness of another night, when he'd walked in on Yinfir drawing the earthy magic out of Ignatius's body. Anger and something else—sorrow tinged with fear—licked at him, burning him worse than the iron ever could.

Lily was vulnerable now. Again, Neer was helpless. A growl escaped his lips. He'd underestimated Yinfir again.

If only he'd drawn his dagger before. If only he'd accepted Yinfir for what he was and not tried to help his friend seek redemption.

After Yinfir secured her, he withdrew a pouch, no doubt full of tiny gems with which to pay the piskie for her services. Neer guessed the piskie's greed outweighed her fear of iron.

The tiny creature swooped down, grabbed the blue pouch, no doubt laden with treasures, and zipped out into the night.

Yinfir paced the small space, keeping his distance from the circle of iron oxide. The red powder lay against the dirty floor, seemingly innocent and yet powerful enough to hold Neer captive. Blood roared in his ears.

He was angrier at himself than he was at Yinfir. Because Neer should've known better.

Yinfir dangled the Ever Key out in front of him, its surface gleaming golden in the fae-light he held in his other hand.

It hung on the long gold chain Neer usually wore around his neck.

"The council—" Neer began.

Yinfir shushed Neer with a wave of his hand. "Can't stop me. I've found a powerful family of witches in a small village in Ireland. With this key, I can break through their defensives. With that power, I can rise to a status no house-elf ever thought possible. First advisor to the Unseelie king."

"The Unseelie won't welcome you into their court, Yinfir. You're a fool if you think otherwise."

"My connections tell me differently. You and I, we just took different paths. And look at you. A disgrace. I, meanwhile, am rising in the ranks of the Unseelie Court."

The house-elves usually aligned themselves with the Seelie fae—the good fae, humans would call them. Unseelie were dark, vicious, unpredictable. They didn't play well with humans.

"I have the key," Yinfir said, pacing, dangling the aforementioned prize out in front of him. "So what do I do with the woman?" He grinned wickedly.

"Leave. Her. Alone," Neer growled.

He kicked at the iron oxide, but all he got for his troubles was a sharp burning sensation in his toes. The circle could only be broken from the outside, and only by breaking it in four places—each of the cardinal directions.

Images rolled through his head, a terrifying picture show of the past and what the future might hold, and he flung a few curses at Yinfir.

Lily struggled against her bindings. Her brown hair fell in front of her face as she thrashed.

Finally, she must've realized she couldn't break free.

She stilled, holding her head high and proud in the face of the monster that had once been Neer's best friend.

Chapter Five

Fae-light cast a golden glow on the dust-filled house. The placed reeked of mildew and rot.

Lily struggled against the ropes that bond her to the rickety wooden chair. Try as she might, she couldn't break free of her bonds.

She wasn't sure what the red powder surrounding Neer was, but she guessed some sort of iron. Whatever it was, it held him prisoner. And if it was iron, she doubted he could break free.

And the cavalry wasn't coming. It was just the two of them against this twisted faerie. But weren't all the fae twisted?

No. She watched Neer, the helpless, angry expression etched into his features. Something told her he was a good man, fae or not. Something told her he cared—the feel of his hand against hers when he'd helped her out of the creek bed, the way he'd brushed a stray hair from her face.

They had to get out of this.

Struggling with the bonds only seemed to make them tighter, so she gave up. She tried to catch Neer's eye, but he didn't take his gaze—okay, his *glare*—off his former friend and current enemy.

Think, Lily, think. There has to be a way out of this.

A thought swam to the surface of her mind. She'd promised her sister no magic, but...well, Daisy couldn't have foreseen this, could she?

At this point, Lily didn't doubt that Yinfir planned to off both of them. If he planned to massacre an entire family of witches, why not kill his sworn foe and his pesky charge?

The trolls had ambushed her unexpectedly. She'd had no dealings with the fae before. The troll dust hit her in the face before she knew what it was. This time was different.

Wheels began to turn in her head. Those sleepless nights since she'd awoken from the trolls' spell had been put to use—reading magical tome after magical tome, filling her head with knowledge so that next time, she wouldn't be so blind-sided.

She'd more than hoped there wouldn't *be* a next time, but here it was.

If Luna Hedgewood were here, what would she do?

Lily wracked her brain, thinking of every spell she remembered from the books by her new favorite author. Most were garden-variety spells—spells for protection, abundance, increased prosperity, or familial health or harmony.

But there had been a spell of undoing.

Maybe that would work. If she could remember it.

It had been a simple spell—a piece of bloodstone, an incantation. She'd brought along the bloodstone because it was said to protect against evil spirits, but it could also be used in that spell, according to the author.

Yinfir slipped the golden chain over his head. The fae-light hovered in the air, casting a yellow glow over the filthy house.

He withdrew a dagger that seemed carved of black rock—obsidian, perhaps? It glinted in the light, promising evil. Lily shivered.

The spell. The spell. The back of the chair was open, and she shifted, trying to subtly reach into her pocket. Inside the iron circle, Neer's face was a mixture of anger and pensiveness. She had to act.

"Who first?" Yinfir asked. He smirked. "No. I know the answer. I'll kill the woman while you watch, old friend."

Yinfir passed the blade from hand to hand, his expression eager.

No time left.

Lily grasped the bloodstone in her right hand and closed her eyes, picturing the words on the page. *"Thread on the spool, yarn of wool, what was done, now undo."*

Tingles spread over her body. A good sign? It had to be.

She felt the instant the knots loosened. Her bonds fell away.

She dove toward Yinfir before he could act. The two of them went crashing into the ground. They fell across the circle of iron, and Yinfir screamed.

He stumbled away, clasping at his arm, which had taken a direct hit to the circle of iron.

"What did you do?" Neer asked. His green eyes were dark.

"A spell of undoing."

"What did I say about messing with magic?"

"Desperate times," she said.

"You have to get out of here."

"How do I release you?"

"Just run," he said. There was urgency in those words.

The house began to shake. That couldn't be good.

"What's happening?"

"You never cast a spell of undoing indoors, Lily. The whole place is coming down. Now, go!"

An ache formed in her chest. She was worried—and not for herself. "Not without you."

His green eyes glinted with some inner struggle. Finally, with a nervous glance at the crumbling ceiling, he sighed. "Break the circle at the four cardinal directions."

She did as he asked. Yinfir's fae-light faded to black, so Neer held out his, allowing her to see in the dark.

The house shook. Bits of plaster rained down from the ceiling. The chair she'd been tied to toppled over. Hurriedly she broke the circle.

She grabbed Neer's hand, for some reason not willing to let go, fearing she'd somehow leave him behind in the collapsing house. The key hung on Yinfir's neck, so close yet out of reach.

Yinfir rose, apparently weakened by landing on the ring of iron powder. A beam came crashing down from the ceiling, landing dangerously close to them.

"Neer, let's go!" She tugged on his arm. He seemed torn. The windows shattered at the force of the shaking. Plaster poured down. How long before the roof collapsed?

With a yank on his hand, she pulled him out the door.

They made it to the edge of the clearing before turning around.

Yinfir stood, his face covered in blisters, holding up his injured hands. He seemed temporarily stunned by his brush with the iron.

He sneered at them from the doorway.

And then the house caved in on itself, roof and rafters and beams tumbling down.

THEY STOOD THERE AS the dust settled. No movement came from the house.

"Is he..." she began.

Neer froze, every nerve ending on edge. It couldn't be that easy. He'd been a fool to bring Lily into the forest.

He should've called the council. But yeah, he resented the council for refusing to release him after Ignatius's death from his oath to serve as a house-elf.

Yes, he was a fool, and he'd let Lily pay the price.

He reached over and pulled a few large pieces of plaster out of her hair. "Come on." He tugged her hand. "Let's go."

They reached the edge of the small clearing where the house stood—or had once stood—when the scent of myrrh swept over him.

He didn't hesitate, pushing Lily to the ground and shielding her with his body just seconds before the energy ball swept over them.

Yinfir wasn't dead.

And he had his magic back.

No. Neer wouldn't lose another charge. He'd hesitated before because of the memories that tugged at his heart—his too-soft heart, Yinfir had always warned him.

Not this time. Picturing Ignatius's face, the boy's flop of brown hair, his clever speech, Neer let his dagger fly.

His aim was true. The bronze blade dug deep into the center of Yinfir's chest. The former house-elf stumbled back, shock widening his icy blue eyes.

"Oh, my friend, what have you done?" he said, grasping the dagger. Even in the throes of death his voice had a taunting edge.

Neer ran to his old friend's side, catching Yinfir as he fell to his knees.

Neer pulled the dagger out. Blood poured freely from the wound. He swallowed, hard.

"I am only sorry that I couldn't save you. You were lost long ago, and I couldn't bring you back. For that I am sorry," Neer said.

Yinfir struggled to speak, but whatever words he struggled for did not form. The light went out of his eyes, the spark of life leaving him as he left this world.

Neer bent over and closed Yinfir's unseeing eyes. "May you find peace," he whispered.

He reached down, slid the golden chain from around Yinfir's neck, and slipped it onto his own.

The Ever Key's magic hummed gently against his skin. A sense of peace came over him, even as he grieved the man Yinfir had once been.

Neer had gotten justice for Ignatius and the boy's family. Perhaps now he could move on, find some comfort in protecting Lily and her family from the fae that roamed these woods.

He turned to Lily. Soon it would be dawn. Had he only known Lily a single night?

He held the fae-light in one hand, offering Lily his other. She tucked her hand into the crook of his elbow, and they made their way back to the house.

He'd kept her safe; he'd found a sense of closure.

Perhaps, finally, he'd found a way to move on.

NEER HELD THE FAE-LIGHT sphere out in front of him and led her through the wood. Adrenaline surged through Lily's veins, keeping the fear at bay. She knew it would be back. It always came back.

But she would face it.

She would get a dagger, she decided. One forged of iron, and she would learn to fight. She would never be caught unawares again.

And yes, if she had to meddle a little more with magic, she would.

Only next time, she'd research more. She'd be more careful. She wouldn't just cast a random spell. Or, worse, two random spells.

A branch snapped nearby, and they both froze. Neer shoved her behind him. She listened like a horse with its ears perked, trying to steady herself, bracing herself for whatever fate awaited them.

A familiar high-pitched laugh greeted her ears, and a shiver swept across her skin.

Trolls.

Not again. She wouldn't be their victim again.

Two trolls stepped out of the shadows and into the glow of Neer's fae-light.

They were only a few feet tall, clad in ratty blue and red garments. Their skin was tan, their faces wrinkled. One had hair the color of a copper kettle; the other's was walnut brown. Their diminutive appearance belied a strength and cunning that she'd underestimated last time.

"You've come back," one of the trolls said, and its high voice set her nerves on edge.

"And brought a friend," the second said in a sing-song voice.

"Leave us," Neer growled.

"We aren't afraid of your kind, house-elf," the second troll said.

"You should be." Fae-light glinted off the bronze dagger Neer clutched, the ruby shining like a beady eye. But she knew that all it took was one dose of troll dust, and the endless sleep could claim them both.

"Go. Now," Neer commanded, steel in his voice.

The trolls laughed. "This is our forest. Here, unseelie reign."

There was a sound of rustling branches.

And then the third troll leapt down from the trees.

The troll landed behind them. She heard its stocky body hit the ground, and she spun around. The trolls had them surrounded.

Lily backed up until her back was pressed against Neer, leaning on his strength.

More than anything she wanted the safety of the farmhouse, to pull the covers up to her chin and quiver beneath the blanket. She wanted to run, to flee and never look back, but she knew she couldn't outrun the trolls.

The panic threatened to blur her vision, to send her stumbling and fleeing through the darkened wood. But she wouldn't give in. She wouldn't let fear dictate her life. She would fight.

The trolls giggled, a sound like a butter knife drawn against a chalkboard, and she covered her ears, fighting the urge to flee.

"Leave this place," Neer commanded, and his voice didn't waver. Something swept over her, like an ocean wave tickling her toes.

Relief.

Not just because Neer was with her.

But because this time, she would fight. She spun the hematite ring around on her finger, drawing strength from the stone, from the unbroken circle of polished black rock.

"This is *our* place," one of the trolls said, menace in his voice.

Neer released the fae-light; it hovered in the air above them, casting golden light over the nighttime forest.

It happened in a blink of an eye. The brown-haired troll lunged forward, and Neer moved like summer lightning. The second troll, copper-haired, dove in after his friend.

Metal clashed and zinged against metal as Neer battled the two trolls with his dagger.

She saw the clash of his dagger against the silver knives the trolls had drawn. They were small, but also agile and strong and wickedly fast.

The third troll eyed her, a glint in its citrine eyes. "Mine again, girly." Goosebumps prickled against her skin.

This was him—the troll who'd doused her with troll dust. The shadows of the forest seemed to close in, reaching for her like incorporeal fingers.

I won't go back to that place.

The last strands of fear threatened to entrap her like a spider's web. She only shook her head, forced the words from her throat. "Not this time."

With all her might, she lashed out, kicking the troll. And then she crash-landed on her arse. It was as if she'd kicked a brick wall.

The troll stood, unfazed, and shook its head.

"This time," it hissed. "Every time."

It reached for the brown pouch at its side. Troll dust.

She rose and backed away until the solid trunk of a wide tree met her back, its bark rough through the thin material of her camisole. Her breath came too fast.

She remembered all too clearly the nightmares, the labyrinth through which she'd wandered seemingly forever, and the horrors that maze of dreams held. She wouldn't go back.

She scurried around the tree and pressed a hand to her chest, her vision blurry, her thoughts filled with images of shadows and earth that threatened to consume.

"Girly, the forest cannot protect you. The forest is ours," the citrine-eyed troll hissed. He stepped around the tree, eyes glinting in the fae-light. He grinned. "You shouldn't have come back."

He dangled the bag of troll dust in front of her, taunting her this time.

One of the trolls battling Neer let out a high shriek, and she spun around the tree to find the brown-haired troll on the ground as Neer pulled his dagger out of the fallen troll's chest.

"Nexie!" the citrine-eyed troll hissed, the brown pouch clutched in his hand as he stared at his fallen friend. His attention shifted to Neer, and rage filled those seemingly glowing eyes.

She hoped that would send the other two fleeing into the shadows, but if anything, they seemed enraged. They let out war-whoops. One charged Neer, flying high into the air and kicking him solidly in the chest. He went down, unleashing a curse and clutching his already injured shoulder.

The troll she'd kicked unsuccessfully held a handful of sparkling green dust. Neer. Her heart raced. She had to do something.

The troll approached Neer, clutching the dust in its tiny hand.

She flew out from behind the tree like a woman possessed. Gathering speed, she ran toward the troll—and then she kicked again, this time with both feet and the force of her momentum.

She hit the ground hard, and the troll shook off her blow. She rubbed her tailbone where she'd hit. Her kicks seemed to be doing more damage to her than the trolls.

Neer flew at the citrine-eyed troll, tackling it. The pouch of dust lay on the ground, shimmering green scattered on the forest floor. She took up the bag.

It was time for payback, she thought, trying to steady her shaking hand as she grasped the bag.

Both trolls were fighting like wild cats, throwing themselves at Neer.

Neer pinned one to the ground, plunging his bronze dagger into its chest. It let out gurgling breaths as it succumbed to the wound.

"Neer," she called. "Fall back."

He stepped into the shadows, and she flung a fistful of dust at the remaining troll.

Shock registered in its yellowish eyes before it staggered. And then, with a sigh, the creature fell to the ground.

Neer rushed to her side. She dropped the pouch and swayed on her feet. Her heart pounded in her chest.

Was it over? Really, truly over?

"Are you all right?" he asked. He brushed her hair away from her face, his green eyes meeting hers.

She could only nod. She allowed herself the weakness of falling into his embrace, allowing his arms to come around her. He smelled like the forest, like the scent of pine and wood smoke, and the muscles of her body relaxed ever so slightly.

"We make a good team," she muttered against the fabric of his shirt. His hands slid up and down her back.

"That we do."

She'd lost something in these woods, and today, with his help, she'd found it again.

Somehow, she sensed they were better together than apart.

Chapter Six

Neer wasn't sure how long he stood there, his arms wrapped around Lily, breathing in the scent of strawberries and coconut, afraid to let go, caught up in some sort of spell that he hadn't felt in a long time.

It felt good. Damn good.

And it shouldn't. She hadn't wanted a house-elf, he reminded himself. And he was certain she hadn't wanted to be dragged into his unfinished business.

No, the best thing he could do for Lily was to wait for the new moon, allow the spell of unbinding to take place, and walk out of her life.

"Come on. We should get back to the farmhouse," he said, withdrawing from the embrace, reluctantly releasing her.

It was the last thing he wanted, he thought as they walked toward the farmhouse, the rising sun tinging the sky shades of gold and mauve.

He allowed the fae-light to dim. Shadows still lurked, but the sunrise brought with it the song of morning birds and the scent of ferns.

She stepped away from him, toward the path that would lead them to the farmhouse. She turned when he didn't move.

"Coming?" she asked, a smile on her face. Beneath the fear, she was bold—maybe a bit impulsive, even. And playful.

His heart hammered his chest.

He could only nod. Something had changed, shifted inside of him, at once imperceptible and monumental.

Lily, too, looked different. Something glittered in her blue eyes, a sort of happiness that hadn't been there before. They were both lighter and fuller at the same time.

Closure, he decided as he stepped toward her. That's what it was.

She stopped at the edge of the forest, staring into the slight valley that held the farmhouse and its sprawling gardens. He paused at her side, the faithful house-elf. If she would have him.

"Lily," he began, his voice coming out strained. He cleared his throat, tried again. "I will try not to be in your way these next few weeks until the new moon."

She turned to her, pressed one hand to his cheek, and smiled up at him. "Is that what you want? To be released?"

He hesitated, bit the inside of his cheek. "Is that what you want?"

She grinned. "I..." She removed her hand and turned to face the farmhouse, fidgeting with a lock of her long brown hair. Finally, chin held high, she turned back to him. "I'm not the same person I was when I entered the forest. And that's because of you."

"I'm sorry," he began.

She held up a hand. "No. Before tonight, I'd lost some part of myself I thought I'd never see again. And you helped me find it. You are a good man, Neer, and you've helped me see the good in the fae and find the strength in myself. If you want me to release you, I will. But if you want to stay...What I'm saying is...Stay. If that's what you want." Her eyes filled with warmth mixed with hope, and he smiled.

He took her hand, extricating it from her hair, and brushed a kiss against her knuckles. He was a house-elf, but he was also a man. With Lily at his side, he could be both again.

"It would be my honor to stay."

She reached up, ran her fingers through his hair. Their eyes met, something soft and yet full of fire, and he couldn't restrain himself.

He leaned in and captured her strawberry-scented mouth in a kiss. Sweetness melted into heat as the kiss deepened, lips parting, tongues exploring, moans pouring from each of them.

Finally, he pulled away. He was far from sated, but he couldn't rush.

He tucked her hand in his and together they walked toward the simple white farmhouse, toward whatever fate held in store for them.

It was a good day—the first one he'd had in a long time.

The Midnight Path
Faerie Spells: Book 3

"The iron tongue of midnight hath
Told twelve lovers to bed; tis
Almost fairy time. I fear we
Shall outstep the coming morn
As much this night we over-watch'd."

William Shakespeare
A Midsummer Night's Dream

Chapter One

Autumn wind howled like a banshee outside the walls of Fairshadow Manor. And for Daisy, that wasn't mere overwrought cliche; she'd literally heard banshees wail, goblins cry, and trolls chortle.

Beside her, Rhett, her husband of six weeks, slept, the steady rise and fall of his chest assuring her his was a deep, peaceful slumber.

Daisy tugged the comforter up. The down-filled linen was crisp yet slightly velvety.

Rhett had told her to go to town redecorating the manor any way she liked. She'd chosen earth tones and touches of pastel to offset the austere and somewhat stoic architecture of the manor. The comforter was sunny yellow with a smattering of gold vines. The sheets were crisp sage-green fabric with eyelet trim. The numerous pillows were feather-filled. Already they'd shared many nights of lovemaking in this bed.

Her marriage to Rhett was exactly what she'd hoped marriage would be: despite the difference in their financial states and family backgrounds, theirs was a marriage of equals.

They both challenged each other to try new things. She'd been ziplining. He'd taken salsa-dancing classes. Their free time was filled with hiking and travel. Their nights were spent sipping tea, often her own creation from the mystical teashop she ran with her sister, Lily, or reading books, or camping in the mountains. Or making love.

But these past few nights, she felt a restlessness. Some unease stirred in her. Sleep didn't come, and when it did, it was fitful, her mind ravaged by nightmares, the hissing of sinister fae folk.

"What does she dream? Not peace," one fae woman whispered.

"War, then," supplied another.

"No, no," the first insisted. "Not war. The battle is long past. But the queen and her laws. The queen..."

"Oh, yes," the other agreed. "We do have rules."

"Rules."

Together, they cackled.

Daisy shivered. Sleep definitely wasn't coming anytime soon. She shimmied out from under the blankets, careful not to wake Rhett. He'd offered to help Lily negotiate with a contractor on installing some light fixtures for the new shop the next day.

She and Lily wanted a brick-and-mortar store to house their ever-expanding business, Tea Thyme. Soon, that shop would be a reality—if they could get everything finalized.

She was not having her notoriously cantankerous husband handling such a delicate negotiation on a poor night's sleep.

Daisy slipped out of the room, leaving a sleeping Rhett to his dreams.

The halls of Fairshadow Manor were wide, lined with wrought-iron lanterns and oil paintings some long-lost ancestor had chosen.

It often made Daisy feel as though she were staying in some sort of castle in the Scottish Highlands, which wasn't a bad thing, except the place needed a few touches of warmth here and there. It was a home, after all, not a museum.

That's where the pastels came in. And the randomly placed milkglass vases filled with flowers. And Daisy was pretty sure she'd bought a grand's worth of cozy throw pillows and blankets. There were bowls of homemade potpourri that she and her Lily had made in August, which made the whole place smell like lavender and wildflowers.

Home. Bit by bit, Fairshadow Manor felt more and more like home.

In the kitchen, Daisy fired up the propane stove to heat the kettle. Though chamomile and valerian was her go-to fair for sleepless nights, tonight she craved a cup of peppermint tea. Or two cups. Or three.

On second thought, she'd better make a whole pot.

Rain splattered against the kitchen windows, wind whipping through the forests surrounding the manor. On over two-hundred acres in the mountains of Foster Springs, Virginia, Fairshadow Manor was the subject of a great deal of local lore, much of it far more steeped in truth than most locals would've dared believe.

The fae walked these woods. Walked. Danced. Chanted. Got up to all manner of sinister deeds.

Upon moving to Foster Springs, leaving behind the house in upstate New York where she and Lily had been raised by flower-child parents after inheriting a quirky farmhouse and tea business from their great-aunt, Daisy had soon learned faeries weren't all pixie dust and garments made of flowers. There were plenty of fae out there who were, well...bad news.

But they couldn't be all bad, could they? She remembered posing the question to Rhett once. Rhett was part fae, after all, and his family had deep roots in local fae traditions. Just how deep, Daisy wasn't even sure Rhett knew. Another mystery for them to sort out together.

Rhett had shrugged. "Haven't met a good one yet."

And thus had ended that conversation. The tea kettle squealed, and she poured the steaming water over the waiting peppermint leaves. The scent wafting up from the steeping tea instantly soothed her, a balm for her soul.

She placed the teapot, her favorite teacup, a jar of honey, and a few snacks on a tray and padded into the sitting room. Smaller and homier than the living room with its big-screen TV, glass-top coffee table, and leather seating, the sitting room featured oil paintings of flowers that Daisy had reclaimed from the attic, along with a Victorian settee reupholstered in deep purple and a selection of velvety throw pillows.

Daisy sipped her tea. If only she could figure out what troubled her, maybe she could ease her mind. If only.

If only...

The tea worked its magic, sip by sip.

As she drifted off to sleep, a soft, sage voice whispered, "When does two make three, my lovely? When does two make three?"

RHETT ROLLED OVER, his arms instinctively reaching for Daisy—and finding an empty bed instead.

He frowned.

Something felt...amiss.

His mother had called it clairsentience. Probably your faerie lineage, she'd assured him, as though that were a comforting thing to hear.

As though, if he'd had a choice, he wouldn't have left any connection he had to the faeries of Foster Springs, Virginia, in the dust.

He and Daisy just returned from spending four weeks in the Scottish Highlands, traveling by train or rental car, staying in quaint bed-and-breakfasts and a rental cottage next to a fallen down castle.

He'd always thought it was Daisy's sister, Lily, who was the hopeless romantic, but it turned out, Daisy had a weakness for all things Scottish. They'd traced her family lineage and down genealogy research, tried and subsequently rejected the taste of haggis, bought their weight in plaid blankets and throw pillows to liven up the dreary confines of Fairshadow Manor, and hiked to gorgeous fairy pools.

On the rainier days, they hadn't, of course, left their room much, leading to knowing winks from hosts and hostesses about "newlywed bliss."

But Daisy had seemed a bit worn out ever since they returned two weeks prior. Not known for a penchant for sleep, she'd slept in, and a few times he'd found her stretched out in a comfy corner in the manor.

Rhett stretched and went to the window, where autumn rain formed patterns against the century-old glass, paned with wrought iron. He couldn't touch the glass itself—the iron would burn his skin—but in the warmer months, he could crank it open.

The iron was a reminder that Fairshadow Manor was both a prison and a sanctuary. The iron kept the fae out of the house, should they be bold enough to try to enter. But it also reminded Rhett that he could never truly leave this place. That was the magic that took root inside of him.

His magic was tied to the Fairshadow Forests, to the mountains and woodlands of Foster Springs.

He sighed, trying to suppress the familiar bitterness that formed a knot in the pit of his stomach.

His life was tethered to this place. He'd warned Daisy. He loved her. He wanted to spend his life with her.

But he didn't want her stuck here in this gothic style manor house, bound forever to a place where fae plotted against humans.

The grandfather clock in the hall chimed five times. Maybe the day could still rise sunny and wash away his gloom. He and Daisy could drive into town, where she and her sister, Lily, were opening up a brick-and-mortar location for Tea Thyme, their tea business. They were expanding and, in addition to selling their tea blends, they'd be selling items like bath salts and herbal tea baths, herbal-infused home remedies, and the like.

Lily was trying to get Daisy to offer tea-leaf readings. She'd eagerly thrust a book in Daisy's face the night before, with a playful waggle of her eyebrows.

Daisy had laughed about it on the car ride home. "Lily is incorrigible," she'd declared.

"Says the woman who met her future husband trespassing on his land," Rhett had replied.

It was five a.m., which meant the European stock exchanges were open for the day. Rhett figured he'd check on Daisy, then hop on his laptop and see if he could find a good trade to make for the day. He had something of a knack for stocks, and had nearly tripled his family's wealth since coming into his inheritance—not a piece of information he shared with many people.

But now, he had Daisy. Sweet, down-to-earth Daisy, whose only request when he finally worked up the resolve to share her his balance sheets had been that he purchase a new roof for the local animal shelter. The old one had been leaking and they needed it repaired before winter, and bake sales weren't exactly raking in the dough.

Stray cats and dogs in a shelter with a leaky roof? Yeah. That request he'd been only too happy to oblige.

He slipped into a pair of khakis and an olive green v-neck sweater before heading downstairs. He found Daisy curled up on the settee in the sitting room. He'd offered her the entire house to redecorate as she liked. His mother had been rather taken with the mystique of Fairshadow Manor, and her decorating touches had only reinforced its bleakness rather than softened it. Rhett had redecorated a few rooms in a more modern style after his parents moved to New York, but many rooms had been untouched.

The sitting room had been a gift to Daisy. Lily had helped him make it as homey as possible. Buttery yellow walls, antique brass candlesticks with beeswax candles, sheer white curtains, and floral prints combined with warm oil paintings of flowers to make the room feel cozy and inviting.

She gave a soft snore, still deep asleep, a half-empty teacup on the coffee table. He pulled a soft blanket in pale green and deep plum and burgundy plaid off the back of a blush velvet armchair and draped it over her sleeping form. Then, he crept away, not wanting to wake his sleeping beauty.

Down the hall, in his study, he powered on his laptop and fired up his imported espresso machine. The kitchen was too far away to be practical for a much-needed pick-me-up while he was trading, so he made sure to keep everything necessary in his office. He fixed himself a cappuccino and unwrapped a power bar while studying the still-dark view outside his window.

Beyond the flagstone patio with its fountain, which even late in the season sent plumes of water in all directions, the forests lurked.

His gut clenched.

Something was coming—coming straight for them.

His hand shook, hot espresso and steamed milk splashing onto his skin. He set it on a nearby table hastily, grabbing a paper towel.

"Dammit," he mumbled, shaking his now burning hand. Not as bad as touching iron, but scalding hot coffee was not exactly a pleasant start to the day.

He slumped into a chair. If Daisy had entered, he didn't doubt she'd comment on his "trademark scowl."

He needed a distraction, and trading wouldn't do. He took a bite of the power bar to ease his now roiling stomach. Across the room sat a box of books Daisy had purchased at a rare-books shop in Edinburgh. They couldn't have possibly brought the books with them on the plane, so the owner had agreed to send them.

They'd arrived the night before, just as he and Daisy were heading into town to do some odds and ends at Tea Thyme, in preparation for the grand opening.

The least he could do, Rhett figured, was unpack them and check the contents against the packing slip. She'd purchased a good dozen books or so, some of them pricey and quite rare—not exactly the sort of thing you could find at your local chain bookstore.

And Rhett himself had purchased a book of collected Scottish folk songs, many of which had been penned by Robert Burns himself, that he was eager to dig into. Whimsy wasn't exactly his strong suit, but he enjoyed folk music and was eager to add the book to his personal collection.

When he opened the box, though, there wasn't a packing slip to be seen. He frowned, taking the old, weathered books out one by one and stacking them on the glass-topped coffee table.

"Of course," he muttered, his grumpiness at the soggy morning only deepening.

There were a couple books on herbalism, one on Scottish folk remedies, another on tasseography—surely a gift for Lily, sure to fuel her new tea-leaf reading kick—and yet a couple more that were collections of folk and fairytales. There were three traditional Scottish cookbooks, an out-of-print fantasy novel that he remembered Daisy saying was one of her favorites, and an old children's picture book about the Fin Folk, a type of Scottish water faerie.

But there was one in particular that caught his eye. And he did not remember either he or Daisy selecting it in the bookshop that day.

Its cover was deep green, like pine boughs, rough and hard-backed. The text was gold, though a bit burnished with time. The cover and the pages within showed substantial wear and tear, and the bindings seemed to be giving way.

But it was the title, in time-burnished gold, that caught his eye, that made his breath hitch.

The Battle of Foster Springs, it read. *A History of the Great Fae Battle Across the Pond.*

Chapter Two

D aisy woke to her stomach churning, her body draped in a soft, warm throw blanket. Despite the unease in her stomach, she couldn't help but smile as she ran her fingers along the fabric.

Rhett. Beneath that gruff exterior was a warm heart. Rhett Fairshadow—whom her sister had once dubbed the "Mysterious Laird of Fairshadow Manor"—was a thoughtful man with a heart of gold.

But when one lived surrounded by unfriendly fae, maybe being guarded about said heart was only natural.

In the kitchen, she fixed herself some dry toast and a cup of peppermint tea. Mint was a hardy plant, and its many varieties grew in abundance in the acres of gardens she and her sister Lily tended.

The deed to the farmhouse was technically in both their names, since their Great-Aunt Mari (short for Marigold) had willed it to both sisters, but Lily currently lived there with Neer, a tall, dark, and handsome house-elf she'd accidently summoned and subsequently fallen in love with that summer.

Growing up, the sisters had been raised by parents who were polar opposites on the exterior, yet twin flames on the inside. Their mother had been a drummer in a traveling pagan folk band when she'd meant her husband-to-be at a local pagan festival in upstate New York. He'd been out of place, she'd said, in his sweater vest and wire-rimmed glasses, an anthropology professor at a local community college with a love for all things based in folk tales, folk remedies, and folk songs.

They'd fallen in love beneath a starry September sky, Camille Devereaux-McAllister said, and married on Halloween. Lily, the eldest, soon followed.

Daisy smiled, staring out the window, where pale mists snaked out from the woods toward the house. The kitchen, with its modern aesthetic, was slowly transforming into a blend of both her more eclectic, rustic tastes and Rhett's refined and modern style. Stainless steel appliances and sparkling granite countertops contrasted with braided rugs and jars of herbs, and she'd added plenty of potted plants and a few crystals—the latter gifted to her by her sister—for good measure.

A blend of both of them.

Two makes three.

"Morning," a gruff voice rumbled from the doorway.

A smile slid across her face as her husband joined her at the window.

He poured himself a cup of tea from the Blue Willow teapot, and they watched the last, most stubborn of the autumn leaves spiral toward the ground.

"Rhett?" she whispered.

"Yeah?" he said, taking a sip of his tea.

"I'm pretty sure I'm pregnant."

He choked on his tea.

She took a bit of her remaining toast crust and rubbed his back, not able to suppress her laughter.

"Smooth," she quipped.

When he'd regained his breath, he gave her a goofy grin, one that he rarely showed. "Are you sure?"

"No."

He started pacing. "We have two options. The room across the hall, though the fae get loud at night, and that might interrupt the baby's sleep. Or we can turn the sitting room in the master suite into a nursery—"

She silenced him with a kiss. "Let's not get ahead of ourselves, okay? We don't know for sure."

He furrowed his brow. "Is this where you tell me to ground myself in the moment?"

"Yes."

He gave her a much longer kiss, which she returned in earnest, warmth spreading through her body. She was tired, sure, but she was still a woman.

They made good use of the kitchen table, and then Rhett carried her back to their bedroom, where they spent the morning spooning under the covers.

RHETT COULDN'T HELP the smile on his face as he eased his luxury sedan into an impossibly small parallel parking spot on Ashwood Street, a street that was an eclectic hodgepodge of shops typical of small mountain towns with endless tourist appeal. An old-fashioned candy shop, a used bookstore, several restaurants that were either town staples or changed hands by the hour, a couple of art galleries and trendy boutiques, and a consignment store.

And there, with its green awning and cursive script, a chalkboard sign out front proclaiming "Opening Soon!" was Tea Thyme.

Rhett had fronted the money, and he was sure people would talk about that, but frankly, Daisy and Lily had a solid business. It wasn't just tea, salves, and Lily's new obsession with reading tea leaves. They'd be selling goods from other local artisans, too, offering an opportunity to sell their wares when the farmer's market was closed. Daisy had a sweet demeanor that made people feel at ease and a good head for business, and Lily had endless energy and could strike up a conversation with just about anybody.

As far as Rhett was concerned, his job was to just step out of the way and let the two of them work their magic.

Lily had covered the windows with brown kraft paper, saying she wanted a big reveal on opening day. She and Daisy had shared a few well-placed hints around town, and between that and the primo location, they were generating plenty of buzz. Their goal was to open in time for Thanksgiving.

He and Daisy had spoken on the car ride over, deciding the holiday would be the perfect time to tell the family their news. Part of Rhett wanted to hide Daisy somewhere far away from Foster Springs—and the clutches of the fae who roamed the surrounding forests—until their baby was born.

His gut clenched.

Because when a Fairshadow child was born, the fae always paid a visit.

A request. That was how it always went. A gift, and a request.

Daisy had taken a test that afternoon, and it had confirmed what she'd told him that morning. She thought not telling her sister would be the hard part.

No. The hard part was what he knew was coming for their unborn child. Faerie magical abilities—whether they wanted them or not.

Daisy, now clad in gray leggings, a navy-blue cardigan, and a patchwork dress in shades of pale blue and mustard yellow, unlocked the front door to the shop.

Lily was inside, standing on a rickety wooden ladder while arranging strings of fairy lights tangled in grapevines and dried leaves. Ambiance, no doubt.

There were tables and chairs for tea tastings and tea-leaf readings, and the walls were lined with shelves full of bulk and prepackaged tea blends; artisan soaps, lotions, salves, and bath salt blends; and goods ranging from hand-painted silk scarves to wheel-thrown pottery to soy candles, all by local craftspeople. One table displayed a mix of local honey, tea blends, and homemade tea cups, along with signed paperbacks by a local mystery writer.

Everything. They'd thought of everything.

"Lily, get down from there!" Daisy chastised her sister.

Rhett helped his sister-in-law step down from the ladder and stepped back to study her work.

Lily frowned and planted a hand on her hip. "Something's missing." Then, seeming to come out of her decorating fog, she turned to him and Daisy. "You two are late." She tapped her wrist as if pointing to an invisible watch.

Daisy blushed and shot him a glance, shrugging. "We lost track of time."

"Uh-huh. I bet you did." She waggled her eyebrows knowingly. "That's fine. I sent Neer out to pick up some more soy candles from Effie Landers. Something tells me they're going to be a big hit for the holiday season. And Rhett, I handled everything with the contractor. Turns out, his wife makes spice mixes, and we'll be selling those, so he cut me a deal on installing the lighting fixtures."

"How do you know he was telling the truth?" Rhett asked. Lily could be a bit soft-hearted sometimes. He'd really wanted to be there to be sure she didn't get taken advantage of.

"Neer could tell. Said the guy was being honest. It's all taken care of."

"Good. Now, before you two start talking about herbs and what-not, give me something to do," Rhett said. The sisters could talk for hours about how to blend ingredients just-so, and he was all too often lost.

Lily sent him into the back to fill some more individual jars with their holiday spice tea blend.

He gave Daisy a peck on the cheek before whispering gruffly in the ear, "Take it easy."

She tucked a strand of brown hair behind her ear before settling in with a clipboard, running down an inventory list with Lily.

He disappeared into the back, focusing on the oddly calming task of filling the jars and applying labels.

But the day turned sour again, rain pounding on the building like a dreary lullaby.

And amid the rain, he felt the magic rise, the hairs on the back of his neck standing on end.

At midnight the path is open. The voice sounded in his head, ethereal and thoroughly fae.

The mists part, the woods wait.

At midnight, walk the path.

He swallowed the bile that rose in his throat.

Not now.

Not already.

He closed his eyes, the room suddenly a hundred degrees, now sweating through his wool pullover.

Can't we have one day, he wanted to beg. *Just one damn day.*

But that, he saw now, wasn't their fate.

Beyond the storeroom, he heard Daisy and Lily's chatter, interrupted by occasional laughter. He and Daisy didn't keep secrets.

So, what would she say when he told her that he'd kept this one?

DAISY SETTLED BACK into one of the chairs in the front room. Evening shadows gathered outside, and she longed to be curled up in front of the fireplace, snuggled under a blanket with Rhett, but she and Lily had a lot of items on their to-do list before the grand opening.

Daisy felt like she'd been exhausted and distracted all day, but she'd managed to brush off Lily's sisterly prying with a casual, "It's nothing. I think I caught something and haven't quite shaken it off."

"Did you?" Lily had asked. "Or is that husband of yours keeping you up past your 9:30 bedtime?"

With a shared laugh, they'd moved on.

They'd dined on sandwiches and minestrone soup Rhett had picked up from their favorite bistro in town, and he'd run out to do a few errands while Lily showed off her new tasseography skills.

The scent of Earl Grey wafted up from the cup as Lily poured steaming tea into a deep blue mug patterned with stars. The inside was white, to allow the leaves to be more easily read.

"Uh, how much have you spent on all of this tea-leaf reading stuff?" Daisy asked.

Lily sat back as they waited for the tea to steep and cool. "Well, there's the cups I ordered from an online shop in Oregon, a few books, some crystals and such to set the mood. Not that much."

Huge chunks of amethyst, smoky quartz, labradorite, and clear quartz bedecked the round table between them, a corner of the shop set apart by dangling fairy lights and gauzy lavender and stormy blue-gray curtains.

Daisy leaned back in her chair, eyeing the stack of books in the corner, a stack that seemed already precarious and constantly growing. She bit her cheek to suppress a grin.

After what had happened to her sister—the endless sleep, the nightmares, the horrors that haunted her—she was glad to see Lily more herself again. A bit impulsive, curious to a fault, and relentlessly enthusiastic.

"Let us begin," Lily said. Clear quartz crystal points dangled at her ears, a piece of raw amethyst hung from her neck on a long silver chain, and she wore a ring on nearly every finger. Except for one—a ring Daisy knew was awaiting a ring pending a certain question from Neer, Lily's fae boyfriend.

Daisy wrapped and oversized pashmina around her shoulders, hoping the tea would warm her.

They placed their hands, palms up, on the table, and Lily played a singing bowl for a moment.

At Lily's instruction, Daisy drank her tea, the taste of black tea grounding her, the slight zing of citrus energizing her. Earl Grey was, as far as Daisy was concerned, the perfect beverage for rainy autumn evenings—those hot apple-cider people could kiss her mystical behind.

Normally, she placed her loose-leaf tea in a tea ball or strainer, but she avoided the leaves as best she could as she sipped. Lily clasped her hands, then, obviously overcome with nervous-slash-excited energy, flipped through the book she'd placed on the table, as if memorizing its contents.

Daisy set the teacup in its saucer with a gentle clink. "Okay, done. Now what?"

"We turn it over to let the last of the liquid run out. When it's upright once more, all will be revealed."

Daisy snickered. "All will be revealed?"

Lily frowned as she turned the cup over to let the leftover tea drain. "You're not taking this seriously."

"I'm sorry. I know it's important to you. But maybe less showmanship next time?"

Lily nodded, rubbing the amethyst nestled against her peasant blouse. "Okay, that's fair. But you're the first person I've read for besides myself. Neer says he doesn't want to know his future."

"Hmm. Maybe there's wisdom in that."

Lily crossed her arms over her chest. "Am I the only one who cares that out there, the future is this great chasm of uncertainty?" She thrust her arms widely, gesturing to the wider world beyond the cozy teashop. "If we can arm ourselves with even a hint of knowledge, why shouldn't we seize that opportunity?"

Daisy reached across the table and squeezed Lily's hand, now resting beside a smoky quartz point. "I guess I never thought of it like before. Let's do this. Read my tea leaves. Tell me my future. Reveal all."

Lily nodded with a look of satisfaction. "That's more like it."

She turned the cup over. Both sisters peered into the cups, in the mess of dark leaves splattered against the white porcelain.

At first, it looked like nothingness, a bit of mess that needed to be tossed in the compost bin. But then, sure enough, Daisy saw shapes in the leaves, though whether that was her sister's overactive imagination rubbing off on her, she couldn't be sure.

Lily squinted into the teacup, her robin's egg blue eyes just a tad darker amidst the twinkle of fairy lights, her brow furrowed, her mouth a scowl of concentration.

"Ah!" she said, quickly glancing down and thrusting a finger onto a book's open page. "I clear see an egg. Oh, that's good news!"

She continued peering. "A circle...do those look like dots to you? Dots could mean there's a baby in your future!" She squealed. "I could be an auntie. Hmm," she said, and Daisy was grateful Lily was too caught up in the book and tea leaves to see her blush. "That reminds me. My knitting skills are *really* rusty."

"And a crown and a crow." Lily studied the page, her frown deepening, her eyebrows a deep V in her forehead.

Daisy leaned forward. "What?"

"Not sure. The crown means the attainment of your highest ambition, but the crow portends bad news."

Daisy's stomach did a little flip-flop. She glanced at her bag lying across the room, the one in which she'd shoved a sleeve of crackers before leaving the house. She swallowed, her throat dry. Something about that felt wrong. "So, I'll achieve my greatest desire, but it will end in disaster?"

Lily paled. "Do you think it means the shop?"

Daisy couldn't answer. She rushed to the bathroom in the back room, her stomach heaving.

She was washing her face when there was a soft knock at the bathroom door. "Daisy, are you okay?" Lily called. "Do you need anything?"

Daisy cracked the door open. "I'm fine. I guess dinner didn't sit well."

Lily studied her. In her tattered jeans, black peasant top, and crocheted teal sweater, with her layers of jewelry, dark hair in a casual braid, she looked every bit the free spirit to Daisy's far more frumpy self.

"You've been acting strange all day," Lily said. "Are you all right? Tell me the truth."

"I'm fine. I didn't mean to worry you." She hugged her sister, the eldest by eighteen months.

"Still worried," Lily said through their hug.

The shop door opened, and Neer and Rhett walked in, Neer saying something about oak leaves signaling a snowier than usual winter, Rhett nodding quietly.

His gaze settled on Daisy. He was at her side in an instant. "What's wrong?"

"My tea leaf reading made her physically ill, apparently," Lily mumbled. Neer slid his arm around Lily's waist. He was dressed in human attire—a black t-shirt with a charcoal gray button down overtop, and a pair of black jeans. Add in the black leather boots and his dark hair, and he looked like a bad-ass biker, not a house-elf from another realm whose job was to protect his human charges—in this case, Lily.

"You do look awfully pale," he remarked.

"Thanks," Daisy said, forcing a cheeky smile. "That's what a girl always wants to hear."

Lily stepped out of Neer's embrace. "Something is amiss. I know the crown and the crow together weren't the best of omens, but, still..."

"It's not—" Daisy began, but Rhett's sudden tight grip on her hand stopped her mid-sentence.

"What crown? What crow?"

Lily stepped through the curtains into her enchanted divination space, and returned a few seconds later with Daisy's teacup. She held it out for Rhett to examine. "You see here. That's a crown. It symbolizes attainment of a goal or dream. And the crow..." She trailed off.

Neer's face was now set at full-powered scowl, and Rhett's usual ruddy complexion was now white as the driven snow.

Daisy glanced between them.

Rhett seized the teacup and stared inside, as though it were a letter that contained bad news.

With a cry, he threw it at the wall, porcelain shattering.

He turned his back to them, facing the papered-over window. Daisy placed her hand on his back. His breath came in ragged, shallow gasps beneath her touch.

"Rhett? Tell me. What is it? The baby?" she whispered, low enough for only them to hear.

The silence stretched. A gust of wind slammed into the shop, rattled the door in its frame.

"In this case, the crown doesn't mean attainment of a goal," Neer said, his voice low, somber.

Daisy turned to him. "What does it mean, then?"

He shook his head, glancing at Rhett, as if waiting for permission to say.

"What. Does. It. Mean?" Daisy growled, her stomach still sour and her mood swiftly turning to match.

"It's her calling card," Rhett said. There was a sorrow in his voice that she'd never heard before.

"Whose?" Daisy managed, her throat dry again.

He turned to her, gazing down with dark, wild eyes—wilder than she'd ever seen, as though pain and terror threatened to unleash a different side of him. "The Faerie Queen."

Chapter Three

Rhett gritted his teeth, trying to steady himself. Daisy's hand flew to her stomach.

Time. He'd thought they had time.

"I don't understand," Lily said, her tone measured. But the way she clasped and unclasped her hands belied her trepidation. None of them wanted dealings with the fae. "What does the fae queen want with you? With any of us? Why now?"

"I didn't think it would be so soon," Rhett said. He gazed down at Daisy, tilting her chin upward. He had to be strong for her. "I'll handle this, I swear. Whatever she asks of us, of our child..."

"Child?" Lily's voice came out in a shriek. "You're pregnant?"

Daisy's lips fluttered upward, however briefly. "We were going to tell everyone at Thanksgiving." She shot Rhett a look.

Lily hugged Daisy. "I won't tell mom and dad, I swear. My lips are sealed."

There was a sparkle in Lily's eyes, one that often hinted at merriment or mischief, depending on his sister-in-law's mood.

"We just found out ourselves. So, yeah, let's not tell anyone yet," Daisy said.

Neer was leaning against a pillar, one boot-clad foot propped up against it, like an elvish James Dean between takes on the set.

His eyes met Rhett's briefly, and he jutted his chin toward him. "Congrats."

Beneath the single word was an unspoken question—a few, no doubt.

What are you going to do about the queen? What does she want? I know you know what she wants.

"No wonder you've looked like you were in need of a thousand naps today," Lily was telling Daisy. "You sit down and I'll make you a cup of tea."

"I don't need anymore tea. I swear. I *could* use a nap, though. But somehow, I don't think I'm getting one."

"You should go back to the manor," Neer said. "I can patrol the perimeter, guard against any of the queen's minions trying to approach."

The house-elf's offer was generous, but not nearly enough. "It's a start." Rhett glanced down at Daisy. "He's right. We should go back to the manor. You can get some rest."

Daisy glared at him, her eyes boring into him, as if they saw the gearing turning in his head. "Neer, could you pull our car around? Lily, would you grab me my things?"

"Sure," Lily said, planting a kiss on Daisy's cheek. "Do you want me to come by later? I made a batch of pumpkin cupcakes. I could bring some by."

Daisy nodded. When the two had disappeared, she poked him in the chest. "Two things: Number one, how could you know something like this might happen and not tell me. And two, whatever the Faerie Queen wants, you're not handling it on your own. You understand?"

A bead of sweat trickled down Rhett's spine. Not because Daisy. He could handle his wife's wrath.

"At some point, the Faerie Queen summons expectant Fair-shadow parents to her barrow," he said. "She offers a gift and makes a demand."

"And if we say no to this demand? If we refuse her gift?"

Rhett's stomach clenched. Despite the coolness of the room, sweat broke out on his forehead. "As far as I know, it's not possible to refuse either."

"And you never thought to tell me this? You understand a lie by omission is still a lie?"

"What? You wouldn't have married me if I'd told you?"

"Of course I would've married you. But I would've liked to have known that the fae would try to interfere with our children. You didn't think I deserved to know that?"

Lily cleared her throat, standing there with Daisy's tote bag and jacket.

The daggers in Daisy's glare assured him their conversation was far from over. She slid into her jacket, hugged her sister, and they stepped into the waiting sedan out front.

"I have to grab some gear from the house, and then I'll be over," Neer assured him, stepping back onto the sidewalk.

Rhett gave him a brief nod.

If only the accords didn't bind him so tightly. If only he and Daisy could've stayed in Scotland forever. He had the funds to travel the world endlessly, but the accords his ancestors had signed with the fae of Foster Springs, Virginia, were clear—and written in blood.

Three-hundred days per year shall Fairshadow feet tread the soils of Foster Springs...

Blood to blood, the oath was past. It was Rhett's turn to carry out the oath, just as it would fall to his child.

The words thundered in his head as they drove down the foggy road toward Fairshadow Manor.

"Rhett, watch out!"

He barely saw the deer in time. Tires screeched against asphalt. The vehicle came to a halt inches from the animal's body.

The creature stopped in the road and looked at them, not with the blinded expression of a deer stunned by headlights, but with a deliberate look.

Her fur was pale, almost white, but shimmering as though speckled with gold dust. Her eyes were amber, like living pools of embers. Wisps of orange and golden light flickered around her body. She stepped into the woods, disappearing amid the oak, ash, and hawthorn.

"Are you okay?" he asked, heart thumping madly.

Daisy nodded, her eyes wide. "That wasn't...normal."

Nothing about this night, this day, was normal.

Nothing about his life was normal.

Nothing about Foster Springs, Virginia, was normal.

"Definitely not," Rhett said, starting forward again, the car moving at grandpa speeds down the foggy mountain road that led to the manner.

"Fae?" Daisy asked, glancing behind them, as if expecting to see the deer reappearing from the trees.

"At this point, let's assume yes," Rhett said. Not any kind of fae he'd ever seen before. "Maybe a messenger from the queen," he mused aloud.

Back at the manor, all appeared undisturbed. He pulled into the basement garage, and they didn't exit the car until the garage door was fully closed behind them. Upstairs, he turned on the gas fireplace in the living room.

Daisy settled under a hand-knitted blanket in the chair closest to the fireplace—an overstuffed leather armchair. He sat on the floor beside her, staring in the flames.

"There's room beside me," she said, patting the chair.

Rhett shook his head.

"Don't do that," she said, her voice soft but fierce. "Don't pull away from me, withdraw into your head. You didn't choose to be born into this."

He picked at the edge of her blanket, wrapping a loose thread around his finger. "I should've told you about the queen. You should've known going into it what the risks were."

She leaned forward. "Let's start over. Because we can't be fighting now. Not when the Faerie Queen is involved. Not when our child's future is at stake. Tell me."

Rhett stood, pacing in front of the fireplace.

"It's usually the eve of the child's birth. The queen requests an audience with the parents-to-be. She gives the child a gift. Mine was, as she put it, 'He will be as the King of Pentacles. Gold shall flow as easily to him as water to the ocean.'"

"That doesn't sound so bad. There's a *but* though, right?"

"There's a demand."

She swallowed, pulling the blanket more tightly around herself before she nodded. "Such as?"

Rhett's blood thundered in his ears, like a stampede of horses. He remembered the warning. "My father told me mine on my twentieth birthday. *And underneath a Beltane moon, both iron and flame shall burn. And before the throne what was never offered shall be, hinge to hinge."*

"We met on Beltane," Daisy said.

He nodded. May Day, or Beltane, as it was known, was the day he feared most. "You see now why I was so protective that night of anyone entering the forest."

"But what does it mean? It's a riddle, of course. And the night we met, you burned your hands on an iron dagger protecting me. And the fae burned me. But the demand...it's unclear. What was never offered? What hinge?"

"That I don't know. My father said there's always a demand. They told him that on my twenty-fifth birthday, he was to leave, to never set foot on Fairshadow grounds again. Mine is less clear."

She rose and wrapped her arms around him. Her small frame fit perfectly into his arms. He just stood there, holding her, taking what comfort he could in her presence.

"I won't let anything happen to you or our child," he said. "I swear it, Daisy."

She pulled far enough out of his embrace to stand on tiptoe and kiss his cheek.

"I know. Whatever we face, we face together. Understand?"

He nodded grimly. "If I could, I would do it on my own. But I suspect even if you agreed to it, she wouldn't."

There were things about this he didn't understand. He'd interpreted Lily's tea-leaf reading to mean the queen wanted an audience with them immediately. But the baby wasn't due for, by his back-of-the-napkin math, for another seven months. Had he misinterpreted, then?

"Let's get some sleep," he said. "You look exhausted."

"I am," she said.

Hand in hand, they went upstairs. The grandfather clock in the hall told him it was only eight-thirty, but frankly, he didn't care. They were showered and in their pajamas by nine.

Daisy opened a romance novel with a kilt-clad man on the cover before she fell asleep, book on her chest. He doubted she'd read a word. He tugged the paperback gently away and set it on her nightstand, then turned out the light.

He knew he should stay awake, keep a lookout, even if Neer was in the woods guarding the place.

But soon, his eyelids felt like they were weighted with lead. Some part of his brain screamed at him to stay awake, but in the end, exhaustion won, and he fell into a dreamless sleep.

IT WAS THE SCREAMING that woke her.

Screaming. Howling. Peels of horrendous laughter sounding from the fields around the manor.

Daisy shook Rhett. "Rhett. Rhett. Wake up!"

She knew he was a heavier sleeper than she was, but damn, could that man actually sleep through the apocalypse?

At the window, she drew back the curtains and peered into the waiting darkness. A full moon, glowing like amber in the night sky, illuminated the darkness.

A throng of fae kind waited in the midnight shadows, some winged, some with horns, some with skin the color of ferns or rough like river birch bark.

Among them, a man with long inky hair was on his knees. From out of the darkness, green eyes peered back at her.

Neer.

Damn it all.

She didn't bother to change out of her striped pajamas, just grabbed an ivory shawl she'd draped over the back of an armchair and raced down the stairs.

"Rhett, hurry! It's Neer!" she called over her shoulder. Surely, even her husband couldn't sleep through the racket the fae were making.

A side door led to a large, flagstone patio. A three-foot tall stone wall was topped with wrought-iron finials. The fae couldn't cross. Daisy flipped on the overhead lights, daunting fixtures modeled on Victorian street lamps in matching iron. Pools of golden light flooded the patio, where wicker furniture was draped in weather-resistant covers for the coming winter.

She slipped her feet into a pair of rain boots and stepped outside, sucking in a deep breath of frosty air.

In one spot, the stone wall parted, giving way to a black metal gate with a symbol in the center. Seeming Celtic in origin, no one in the family or in town seemed to know what it meant.

Daisy stepped forward, clasping the gate in her hands and gazing at the waiting horde of fae.

"What do you want?" she demanded.

An elven man stepped forward. Tall and proud, his skin pale, his hair platinum with a hint of wintry blue, his eyes just as cold, he glared down his hawk-like nose at her.

"Queen Roisin sent a messenger," he said. "She requests your presence. At midnight the veil will thin, the path will be illuminated under the harvest moon. Follow the trail to her barrow." His eyes narrowed into tiny pinpricks of disgust. With a sneer, he added, "And keep your house-elf off our land. Next time we won't return him in one piece."

He added a haughty sniff at the word *house-elf.* The other fae holding Neer tossed him toward the gate. He hit the wall, screaming as his body scraped the iron finials.

The fae messenger and his friends didn't stick around to wait for her answer. They disappeared as quickly as they'd arrived.

Daisy thrust the gate opened and helped Neer into the house, careful not to get him too close to the iron. Even Rhett, whose fae blood was very much diluted, couldn't have contact with the iron, but it was the best way the Fairshadow family had figured out to keep the fae from entering the manor itself.

"God, Neer, what happened?"

He shrugged. "I tried to call. Called Rhett's phone three times to warn him the fae were coming. When he didn't answer, I engaged. House-elf's duty. Protect my charge."

She helped him out of the leather jacket he was now wearing, carefully to avoid further injury.

"I'm not your charge. Lily is. I mean, she's the one who summoned you."

"You're her kin," he said, wincing and moving his shoulder in a circle, as if testing the damage. The curse he muttered suggested it wasn't pleasant.

"I can manage," she said. "Now, come on. I have a healing salve that will speed up the recovery process."

He glared down at her, his expression thoughtful. "You and your sister are both wise and foolish in your own ways, you know."

"How's that?" she asked, leading him through the darkened hallways of the mansion.

"Lily is outwardly bold, but inside, she holds a great deal of fear. You, on the other hand, pretend to be practical, rational, measured, composed. But I secretly think you are the more impulsive one."

Daisy closed the kitchen cabinet harder than she'd intended, wincing at the hard thwack of its slam in the otherwise quiet house.

Neer chuckled. "I think I struck a nerve."

She didn't respond to his goading, instead pointing at a stool at the kitchen island. "Sit."

Asking him to remove his t-shirt seemed too painful a request, so she cut it from the back with scissors.

Underneath, where his shoulder had brushed the iron, his skin was red and blistered, already oozing clear liquid. Her stomach churned.

Neer glanced at her. "I can manage."

"No. It's..."

"I'll go in the bathroom and clean it. Don't worry. Not my first battle wound. Not my last."

He grabbed the small metal tin of salve and headed down the hallway before she could protest.

Tea. She needed all the tea. She turned on the electric kettle and added a mint tea blend—winter mint, chocolate mint, and spearmint—to the teapot.

"What the hell did I miss?" a voice rumbled from the entryway.

Daisy spun around. Rhett stood there, clad in dark gray sweatpants, a hunter green t-shirt, and a pair of warm wool socks, long blond hair tousled from sleep.

"Her royal highness requests our presence in the forest at midnight," Daisy said, the words dripping with bitterness. "And Neer can't patrol here anymore."

She gulped. Neer was a bit rough-and-tumble, sure, but he was also fiercely loyal, and that tough-guy exterior hid a heart of gold.

Rhett raked his hands over his face, as if trying to dislodge the cobwebs. "Shit. That's a lot. Is he okay?"

"Nothing a little healing salve won't fix." She lowered her voice. "This time."

He nodded. They didn't need anymore words. He understood. "I don't know why I didn't wake up. It was like...a spell or something."

"Not fae, right?" she said, the hairs on the back of her neck rising, cringing at the sharpness in her own voice. "I thought their enchantments couldn't breech the manor's walls?"

"No." But his gaze turned to the forest lurking beyond the window, past boxwood hedges and rose bushes trimmed way back for the winter. "I don't think that's possible."

The kettle chimed, and she poured steaming water into the teapot. "I'm starting to wonder if we even know what's possible."

He kissed her cheek. She leaned into him. He smelled like the body wash she'd made for him, a mixture of cypress and frankincense essential oils. She snuggled deeper into his embrace, his arms encircling her.

The clock chimed. She counted each chime. Eleven.

"One hour," she whispered.

"Silver lining," he whispered against her hair, his arms tightening around her. "We have an hour. We've had less time than that to plan before."

She didn't respond—couldn't, frankly, past the lump in her throat.

Footsteps padded in. Neer returned, having shedded the remnants of his tattered shirt.

Rhett helped him cover his injured shoulder with gauze, then went to grab him a spare t-shirt. Meanwhile, Neer called Lily.

Daisy swirled honey into her teacup, sipping a beverage that had so often steadied her, calmed her, grounded her.

But tonight, the stakes were higher than they ever had been.

And nothing, not even a perfectly brewed cuppa, could drown out the fear that quivered inside her.

Chapter Four

"Lily, stop pacing. You're making me dizzy," Daisy muttered, rubbing her fingers in small circles on her temples.

Fifteen minutes until midnight.

They were all sitting in Rhett's study, surrounded by books on fae lore and a newly acquired book on something called the Battle of Foster Springs—a battle that none of them had ever heard of.

"I mean, it's odd, don't you think?" Lily mused, nonstop. Daisy was beyond wondering how her sister had so much energy this close to midnight. Lily called midnight her "power hour." "Neither of you remembers buying the book, yet there it is. Curiouser and curiouser..."

Lily had plucked one of the wooden stir sticks from a container on Rhett's desk and was gnawing on it. She plopped into a leather chair in the corner, leaning forward, her eyes flickering with the gleam of a thousand ideas.

"We're running out of time," Rhett said, a growl of frustration in his words as he glared out the window.

"What if you don't go? You and Daisy stay in the manor until the baby comes. I can bring you everything you need," Lily said.

Daisy shook her head. "No. I won't be a prisoner to the fae. I just won't."

Whatever the queen wanted with them, Daisy would meet this woman head on.

"Daisy's right. Staying locked up here isn't the answer," Neer said. "Besides, the queen would find a way. The unseelie fae always do."

Unseelie. Which loosely translated meant *unlucky, unfortunate, unholy*.

Daisy shivered and drew her shawl around her.

"Let's focus on the book then," Lily said. "Rhett, what do you remember from reading it this morning?"

Rhett turned back. He'd changed into a gray wool sweater and a pair of khakis, his blond hair in its customary ponytail. He wasn't wearing his contact lenses, so he had on a pair of wire-rimmed glasses that made him look like a hot-professor type.

He removed his glasses and pinched the bridge of his nose. "The seelie and unseelie fae—essentially, light versus dark—waged a battle here. Both sides were devastated. A group of humans got caught up in the battle, and one of them struck a bargain to save the human town. Upon the site of the bargain, a grand estate was built—presumably Fairshadow Manor.

"And the human town was renamed Foster Springs. Foster means 'guardian of the forest.' The human descendants of this man would guard the forest—the place where the pathway between the human and fae realms existed. But the unseelie fae were free to come and go as they chose.

"Except..." He paused, brow furrowing in deep lines as if trying to recall some important piece of information.

Daisy leaned forward in her chair, the blanket she'd draped across her lap falling to the floor.

"There was a prophecy." He grabbed the book from the table and flipped through.

Each tick of the clock grated on Daisy's nerves as she waited. In a few minutes the path would be illuminated, and they'd face Queen Roisin.

Dread coiled like a hissing serpent in Daisy's gut.

"Here." Rhett stabbed his finger against the page, the paper yellowed with age, a thick cream turned slightly brown by time.

"And there will be sisters three
And their kin to make them four
Queens, each, respectively,
The Sword, The Cup, The Coin, The Wand,
And through them the Accords will come undone."

Lily leaned forward, an ah-ha look on her face. "That's a tarot reference. There are four suits—swords, wands, cups, and pentacles. And pentacles are also called the coins suit in some decks."

"So, the tarot is going to undo the accords Rhett's ancestor made with the fae? How does that work?" Daisy asked.

Lily shrugged. "Sisters three? Who is that? There are only two of us, so we know it's not us."

Neer cleared his throat. "If the queen wants to see you, this might be why. It's possible the prophecy is a reference to your unborn child. Or, maybe, children."

Daisy's hand went to her belly. She shook her head, unable to comprehend that a person who wasn't even born yet could be part of some ridiculous fae prophecy.

"We don't know that," Rhett said, seeming just as skeptical. "There's no telling who the prophecy refers to, or if it's even real, or if it would come to pass—or when, for that matter. For all we know, this book was sent here to mislead us."

Daisy glanced at the clock and rose, brushing herself off. She'd put on a pair of sturdy hiking boots, a pair of warm black leggings, and a flowy t-shirt dress printed with daisies underneath a chunky cardigan.

"Rhett's right," she said. "But it doesn't matter right now. Because it's time."

"Let us come with you," Lily insisted.

Daisy shook her head. "No. This is my journey, and Rhett's, our path to walk together."

She hugged her sister tightly. "Don't worry. I don't think the queen will harm us." Inside, her stomach twisted. *Not tonight, anyway.*

What if the prophecy was real—or the fae queen believed it was? What if she didn't want the Accords that bond Rhett's family—now Daisy's family too—to the fae?

Maybe the danger was far more real than any of them realized.

Daisy slid into her jacket. Lily grabbed her for one last hug. "Take my bag," she whispered.

Daisy spared the contents a quick glance.

Her lips quirked in a brief smile. "Clever," she whispered.

Daisy slipped the messenger bag over her shoulder, and then she and Rhett exited the manor, its gothic spires stretching toward the impossibly large moon in the sky.

The veil of fog had lifted. Stars glittered above them, their breath coming out in poofs of white in the cold air. Daisy belted her coat around her and squeezed Rhett's hand.

"Look," he whispered, his voice rough.

At the edge of the woods, the white doe waited. Her eyes met theirs, an aura of magic shimmering around her.

Hand in hand, they followed her toward the waiting midnight path.

Above them, stars glittered, seeming impossibly bright, the way they seemed on a clear winter night on a mountaintop, far from everyone. The scents of autumn leaves and forest detritus mingled with other scents—a touch of oakmoss, the slightest hints of lavender and wild mint, not entirely in keeping with the season. But they were surrounded by fae magic, after all, so anything was possible.

And then the forest seemed to shift and quiver beneath their feet. Rhett grabbed her arm and pulled her against him.

The earth quieted.

"Oh my god," Daisy whispered, unable to keep the wonder out of her voice.

Blue and golden lights twinkled along the path, like strings of fairy lights draped along branch and bracken and tangled along the forest floor. Except these lights seemed sentient, bits of pure magic shining in the night.

The air tingled along Daisy's skin, like a prickle of summer warmth. She stepped out of Rhett's grasp, her sense of caution loosening.

"This isn't what I expected," she said.

She turned to her husband. Rhett's mouth was twisted in a frown of confusion, mixed with worry...and a hint of...surprise, maybe?

"It feels different," he agreed, nodding.

She held out her hand, testing the air the way one tested for impending summer rain. "It feels..." She struggled, searching her brain for the right word and coming up empty.

"Light?" Rhett finished for her.

She nodded. "Light," she said.

The doe looked back, waiting for them.

"The fae can cast powerful illusions if they want," Rhett whispered in her ear.

She swallowed hard, nodding. "I know."

Daisy remembered the terrifying nightmares Lily had suffered under the effects of the troll dust—nightmares that still haunted her sister.

Two parts of her warred as they followed the doe down the wending forest path. On the one hand, part of her wanted to lose herself in the wonder, in the magic of this place—neither of her world, nor quite fae, but some lovely in-between.

And the other, the one that knew what the fae were capable of, wanted her to steel herself against any danger. She'd known better than to bring any iron to visit the faerie queen. That, Neer had confirmed, would've been quickly found and a cause for unspeakable torture.

No. She'd come unarmed to visit Queen Roisin, as had Rhett.

Well, mostly unarmed.

For better or worse...

Who would've thought such a vow would involve midnight meetings with fae royalty?

The tingle against her skin grew, and they approached a mounded hillside speckled with green moss and pale quartz—clear, but with enough silica content that it was striated with white inside.

The mound grew, writhing in front of them until an arched doorway of blue wood formed. It opened with a whooshing sigh, like a potion bottle too long corked, an enchantment escaping upon opening.

The doe glanced back at them and then bounded into the forest.

Daisy stepped forward.

"Wait!" Rhett called. She turned to him. He appeared frozen in fear. "We shouldn't. We should turn back."

Daisy glanced at the doorway, magic shining from within, beckoning. She cupped his cheek. "Trust me. I want to be curled up in bed, fast asleep. But this is where we have to be. We have to trust that many of your ancestors have walked this path before. Tonight is our turn." She stood on her tiptoes and kissed his cheek.

He returned the kiss, brushing one against her temple. "For our daughter," he whispered.

She felt her eyebrow quirk sharply upward. "Daughter? You sound confident."

He shrugged. "Somehow, I just know."

Why bother asking how he knew? When you were married to a man with faerie blood in his veins, sometimes you just had to go with the flow a bit.

The door groaned, as if to say, *hurry up*.

"For our daughter, then," she agreed.

They stepped through the doorway.

THE DOOR SLAMMED BEHIND them with a resounding thud that echoed down a long tunnel of packed earth bathed in golden lantern light. Rhett cringed.

No turning back. And worse, no escape route.

His inner faerie magic, dim though it was, felt different here—stronger, perhaps, and somehow he knew this wasn't just some hidden faerie tunnel.

They were in another world.

The energy of this place wasn't the energy of the forest fae, wild and feral and, frankly, unsettling.

It reminded him of a babbling brook—far from stagnant, but peaceful at its core.

Yeah, the doe with her glowing aura of magic, the flickering of teeny-tiny will-o-the-wisps had a certain spellbinding quality—and he was definitely a cynic in the realm of all things magical. Even Lily's dabbling in tasseography left him feeling a bit queasy.

Daisy tugged the messenger bag flung over her shoulder so it draped over her belly. Worry flickered across her features in the dancing shadows of the tunnel. The enchanting path of fairy lights behind them, reality was hitting them both.

He'd had enough magic to last a thousand lifetimes. The last thing he needed was more.

But here he was.

A gift. And a demand.

The Fairshadow curse.

"What do you think she wants with us?" Daisy whispered as they crept forward. The tunnel was nothing but earth and roots and gray stones, lit by the glow of spherical lanterns with a pale yellow light, and her words echoed against the walls.

"I don't know. Just don't...we can't trust anything. Not even our own senses. Not tonight. Not here, in this place."

Rhett balled his fists. Everything the fae did was a trap. What he felt wasn't the true energy, he reminded himself, but a sort of enchantment. Tonight would be like a masquerade ball, no doubt, fae hiding their true faces and true intentions, but sinister intentions lurking always underneath.

No being lured into a false sense of complacency. No making deals with secret loopholes that served only the fae.

The tunnel ended at a doorway draped only in emerald vines tangled with vibrant moss.

Rhett's stomach turned, bile rising.

"I'll go first," he said. Before Daisy could protest, before his better judgment reared its sensible head, he parted the vines and stepped through.

The scent of moss and ferns, wildflowers and woodsmoke hit him. In the corner, a fae woman played a violin, the notes blending smoothly together to create a song that spoke of sadness without needing a single word.

Lanterns and string lights draped from mossy-clad branches full of verdant leaves. Long tables were cloaked in gauzy white fabric, spread with every kind of fruit one could imagine, along with bundles of fresh herbs and loaves of bread in varying shapes, all arranged artfully amid scattered flower petals and candles in tall, silver candlesticks.

The space was oddly empty, save for the violinist, whose glowing green eyes, fiery red lips, and pointed ears suggested either a fae lineage or an award-winning cosplay getup.

The woman finished her song, her eyes meeting Rhett's. She bowed. She wore a simple garb—a long, rosy pink skirt and cropped ivory peasant top trimmed with lace, a matching lace choker tied around her neck. Her hair, the color of lilacs mixed with a storm cloud, was cut short so that it framed an angular face.

When she smiled, she flashed him teeth that were pointed, like a shark's. Rhett took a step back, stumbling into Daisy.

"Again, unexpected," she whispered. He wanted to glance back at her, but didn't dare take his eyes off the musician.

Daisy stepped around him, curtseying to the violinist, who held bow and instrument poised at her sides.

The musician inclined her head.

"We're here to meet with Queen Roisin," Daisy said. "She's, uh, expecting us."

Without uttering a single syllable, the woman disappeared.

Daisy paced around the table, studying the spread. "It's odd, isn't it? Like someone planned a party but no one came?"

They both knew enough not to eat the feast, whomever it was meant for. Fae could enchant food, and he wouldn't put it past the fae queen to do so. Not that he'd ever met her, but still.

"It's almost sad," Daisy continued.

"I don't know about sad. It is odd, though. I don't think this was meant for us." Rhett stroked his chin. "So, then, who?"

"Representatives from King Oberon's court," a voice interrupted.

Rhett spun around so quickly he nearly smacked into a stone pillar that held a vase of orange tiger lilies and crimson roses.

Some instinct he couldn't explain took over when he saw her. He fell to one knee, bowing his head.

"Your highness," he said, almost by compulsion.

"Rhett," Daisy said, shaking his shoulder.

Somehow, he managed to glance up, past a long, gauzy black skirt and arms covered in tattoos of black, twisting, thorny vines—to finally meet the eyes of the faerie queen.

She was *not* what he'd expected.

Chapter Five

D aisy had expected a pale, gaunt woman clad in otherworldly attire—layer upon layer of silk and chiffon, perhaps a few gaudy jewels thrown in for good measure.

But this woman? She looked like she belonged on the cover of a fantasy novel.

Her hair was auburn brown, flowing to her waist, two sections in braids that were secured at the back of her head. She wore a simple black skirt that skimmed her bare feet, a red tunic top, and a belt of brown leather tooled with strange symbols. A knife with a curved blade dangled from one side. From the other, a small black pouch hung heavy against her thigh.

And as for jewels? Aside from a simple amethyst point on a silver chain, she wore none.

Lips stained the color of rusty red curved up in a smile. Her face was almost painfully pretty—and her eyes, full of both wisdom and pain. She didn't look older than forty—but with the fae, looks could be (and usually were) deceiving.

"I apologize," the queen said with a smile. "This is where the door opens. As for the feast, I'm expecting the king's court at the hinge between day and night."

"Humans call that dawn," Daisy said, shifting her stance. This queen didn't look like she spent much time sitting on a throne being fanned by palm fronds. More like she knew her way around a blade.

Not the sort of woman one crossed, fae royalty or not.

Queen Roisin chuckled. "Yes, I'm aware. But it's been millennia since we've mingled regularly with humankind—and over a century since my people have done so."

"Your people?" Daisy asked. It was too late, and there were far too many riddles and oddities that didn't add up. "The ones who live in the forest?"

She bit her lip, smart enough not to add, *and torment the people of Foster Springs*? Though, oh, how she wanted to let the sarcastic retorts and sardonic barbs fly.

Just not as much as she wanted to return home, knowing the ones she loved most were safe and sound.

Queen Roisin's face soured. Daisy took a step backward, bracing herself.

"Those are *not* my people," she said, an edge to her voice like a long shard of broken glass.

"Then whose are they?" Rhett said, a subtle hint of challenge in his voice.

The queen gestured to an area behind the tables with their abundant and festive spreads. A tent of gauzy white fabric waited. "His. This way. I'll explain."

We are going to die. She pulled her messenger bag tighter to her body as the warrior queen led them into the tent.

Inside were wooden chairs with high backs, upholstered in royal blue fabric. One was more ornate, arms and legs carved in intricate patterns of vines, stars, and moons with strange symbols mixed in.

A throne. An honest-to-god freaking throne.

They sat in the chairs facing the queen, who leaned against one arm of her chair, legs crossed with an air of confidence and familiarity—the sort of woman used to barking orders and seeing them carried out.

Daisy's whole body shook. The air smelled of candlewax from the black tapers flickering in their silver candlesticks. There were crystals everywhere. Lily would've been in her glory—menacing fae aside, of course.

Daisy inhaled, trying to steady herself.

Queen Roisin snapped her fingers. A small creature appeared, his skin weathered and brown, like an acorn or a fallen leaf, his eyes brilliant green set amid his wrinkles.

"My lady," he said, bowing.

"Bring me the box I requested, please," she said. He scampered off, his movements surprisingly spry for such a short, stout creature. Hobgoblin, perhaps? Daisy would have to look into it later. There were so many different types of fae.

The queen reached to a table at her side and took up a pack of cards. She began to shuffle them as she stared at Daisy, then at Rhett, those sharp eyes seeming to miss nothing. If she'd had the ability to transform herself into a dragon, Daisy wouldn't have been surprised.

A gift. A gift and a request of Daisy's unborn child—her unborn daughter. Daisy's gaze fell to the cards, to the impossible dexterity and speed with which the queen shuffled.

Finally, the shuffling stop. The queen fanned the cards and held them out. "Each of you, draw a card."

"No," Rhett growled. "We came as you requested. We know why we're here. It's not for a tarot reading."

The queen's dark lips drew upward in a smirk. "As you wish. I already know the answer."

Daisy shivered.

She did not like the sound of that.

The queen held out the cards to Daisy. She shook her head and gazed down at her bag.

"Ah," the queen said—as though she knew the contents of the messenger bag.

Lily's idea had seemed clever at the time. What was something that wouldn't anger the queen or make enemies of her people, but that would give Daisy some sort of magical advantage?

Right now, Daisy doubted she had the upper hand, but it had been worth a try.

The queen set down the deck and waved her hand as if dismissing their refusal of the reading.

The hobgoblin came back in, handed the queen a flat wooden box of dark, almost black polished wood, and disappeared as quietly as he'd come.

"You refused the reading, but surely you won't refuse a gift? Two gifts, really. One, of material and magic. The other, of words and truth."

Daisy and Rhett locked eyes. Dealing with the fae was never simple. The most innocent of such deals could go horribly wrong. And this wasn't even about them—it was their child's fate at stake.

Rhett turned back to the queen, his voice low, each word sounding crisp and carefully measured. "We accept first the words and truth. The other we haven't decided yet."

Queen Roisin nodded. She set the box next to the tarot cards, freshly shuffled, yet unread.

"The truth is a story—the story of a battle lost, and a prophecy of another yet to come."

RHETT'S ENTIRE LIFE, he'd been avoiding this moment. And now that it was here?

Nothing but a series of images flashing in his mind. That night in May when, under a full moon, a beautiful brunette had snuck into the Fairshadow Forest seeking a mystical cure for her sister.

And then, a thousand stolen moments that followed, all leading to this one.

And behind that, a backdrop. A mother who'd loved the magic and mystique of what she called the family's *eccentric, fairytale past*. A father who'd clasped his son's shoulders that day he'd passed the torch of guarding the forests. A fop of gray hair falling over his father's forehead as he'd met Rhett's eyes with a look that was gloom mixed with resignation and a substantial amount of relief.

"If you don't marry, it ends with you," he's said. And then he'd picked up a weathered gray suitcase and, with one last look, retreated to New York City, where he and his wife would start their next chapter.

Rhett hadn't told his father about the wedding, about Daisy. His father had a bad heart, and he didn't want to add to the strain. But a grandchild? No. His father had a right to know.

Daisy sat on one of the high-backed chairs facing the dais where the queen sat—like Boudicca herself, Roisin was a warrior queen, fierce and strong and seemingly uncompromising.

If there was ever a fae not to cross, it was Queen Roisin. Her eyes met his, glinting like sparks flying from flint in the shadows and lantern light.

"I can't change your mind about that reading?" she asked, her lip quirking ever so slightly as she asked—not quite a smile, a gleam of something enigmatic gone before it truly appeared.

"The story will do for now," he grunted, sitting down next to Daisy. Her skin was pale, her lips drawn in a tight, resolute line, but there was as much steel in his wife's spine as there was in the queen's—of that, he had no doubt.

"Make yourselves comfortable," she said.

She rose from her throne and, to his surprise, began to pace, as though the words she was about to speak left her agitated.

She balled her hands together, unclasped them, braced them at her sides and tilted her head upwards, her lips moving wordlessly. Sparks seemed to flicker around her.

"It was over two-hundred years ago," she began. "Foster Springs was little more than a settlement at the time, a couple-hundred humans living there.

"And we—we'd followed them. My father, King Rhys, had said we should follow the humans to the New World, and make a place for ourselves.

"So we came, the seelie fae. And they came too. The ones who dance in the forest." Her eyes glittered with hatred, a pure malice.

"The unseelie. Years passed, and we tried to live in balance as we had before. But our people had found a place where the magic was pure, where clear waters flowed into a crystalline pool, and the trees were old and ancient, and the earth sang. One night...One night they came to the place where we slept, in tents much like this one.

"And they killed my father while he slept. His guards betrayed him. I ran, I and others, we ran into the forests. The following night, we attacked. This battle went on until one night, a group of human men followed our cries into the forest.

"They watched us battle, hidden among the trees. And when the unseelie found them, they slaughtered those they could reach. The seelie—I was their leader now that my father was fallen—I told them no, leave the humans."

Her voice broke, as if in remembering grief washed over her anew. "And when the dawn broke, a man came. His face was stern, but handsome. He gazed upon me, and I had no doubt he knew what I was. And the unseelie king, Oberon, he was there too.

"'*Leave this place*,' he'd hissed. And I remember..." Roisin sniffed, seeming to take a moment to gather herself.

"I remember the human man, mere mortal. He held himself so proud, so tall, and he said... 'I am the guardian of this land, these springs. The humans too believe in their healing properties. We won't be driven from here.'

"Both sides had lost so much. We couldn't bear to battle another day, another night. And so the Faerie Accords came to be, and the Battle of Foster Springs ended. And the unseelie dance in the forests, an uneasy existence to this day.

"And my people...we live in the barrows, under the earth. And we wait for a prophecy that came to me not long after I met that man, Aberforth Fairshadow. On the night his son was born."

Her eyes locked with Rhett's. He shivered, as if he'd seen what she'd seen, her grief and loss washing over him.

She wasn't the unseelie queen, then, but the queen of the seelie fae. And a battle long ago had left their destinies forever entwined.

Roisin smiled, but there was no joy in it. She took up the shallow box, opened it, and tilted it toward him.

"These were forged of silver and crystals, faerie magic and spellcraft long ago. And they've waited.

"You see, I'm a seer too—among other things. And every time a new descendent of Aberforth Fairshadow comes along, I'm able to give them a gift.

"There will be three sisters, and a fourth, the sisters' kin—but not a Fairshadow. She will not be Aberforth's kin, but she will be fae." Her gaze traveled to Daisy's face. "Your sister, perhaps? I hear she's taken a faerie lover. Neer, they call him. We don't leave the barrow—haven't, not in over two-hundred years—but word still reaches us. It has its ways."

Rhett had sworn whatever that box contained, he wouldn't accept it. No more accepting gifts on behalf on unborn Fairshadow children. It seemed a reasonable enough request, didn't it?

Inside, were four gemstone pendants, each with a round bit of polished stone set in silver shaped in twisting Celtic knots, dangling from a thin silver chain. One, pale purple amethyst;

another, a blood-red ruby; the third, a gleaming emerald; and the fourth, the bluest of sapphires.

Each one glittered with faerie magic—a promise of a destiny entangled with the fae.

The spells, seeming like a thousand incantations, swept over him, the hairs on the back of his neck standing up, goose bumps rising on his arms.

"No." It was Daisy's voice that broke the spell on him.

She stood, clutching her bag.

Queen Roisin looked taken aback. She snapped the box shut with a sharp clap. The magic dissipated, like a bit of rain storm fading away. "You refuse my gift?"

Rhett stood, taking Daisy's hand. He wanted to draw her aside, to warn her of the danger, but a quick glance between his wife and the queen assured him that wasn't possible.

Daisy squeezed Rhett's hand, as if to say she understood the risk. Then, she released it and cross her arms over her chest.

She stared up at the queen. "The girls should decide for themselves. When they're grown, they can each come to you, and you can offer the amulets to them. It's their choice, not ours."

"It's written in the stars," Roisin said, her tone a bit, well, patronizing.

"Then it won't do any harm to wait," Daisy countered, undaunted.

Roisin slid into the throne, tapping her fingers on the polished wood.

The silence stretched. Rhett thought he might be sick.

The queen smiled. "I will consider this. But first, I want to try *your* gift."

"My gift?" Daisy asked, sounding a bit stunned.

"Yes. The one you've brought in your pack."

Chapter Six

U*h-oh.*

Daisy took a step back, clutching the messenger bag tighter.

Who would've guessed the faerie queen was a seer?

Not even Lily with her crystals and tea leaves could've seen that one coming.

Daisy steeled herself. She'd just made an awfully big ask of a faerie queen. And the woman had been trapped in a faerie barrow for hundreds of years, so it stood to reason she wasn't in a mood to grant requests.

The image of those four amulets was emblazoned in Daisy's mind. Four amulets. For four girls who would grow up to be entangled in faerie magicks in ways she couldn't imagine.

But what if her daughter—or daughters—could change the world?

She'd have to raise them to be ready.

Daisy cleared her throat. "I'll need a table."

Queen Roisin quirked an eyebrow.

"Your highness," Daisy added hastily.

Roisin smirked and snapped her fingers, a plume of green sparks rising as she did so. Oh, yeah, powerful didn't begin to describe her.

Out of the corner of her eye, Daisy caught Rhett shifting his stance, crossing and uncrossing his arms.

All I need is a secret weapon that isn't a weapon, she'd said earlier that night. And Lily—fierce, clever Lily—had come up with an answer to that riddle.

The hobgoblin returned and rearranged the furniture, placing a high, narrow table between Roisin's throne and where Daisy now stood.

"Thank you," Daisy said.

He shot her a nasty, withering look.

"It's customary not to thank the fae, human," he muttered.

"I'm..." she started to say, but he was already gone. Just as well. If he didn't like thanks, how would he take an apology?

"Well?" Roisin said, her slender arms crossed over her chest.

"Almost ready...your majesty." The phrase came out awkward, and she heard Rhett's half-snort as he no doubt bit back a laugh.

She sent him a glance. Of course, in this whole situation, *that* was what brought out her husband's sense of humor.

Daisy opened the messenger bag and, hands trembling, removed the contents.

The tea tin.

The teacup and saucer, wrapped in layers of soft fabric to protect them on the journey.

The book: *A Beginner's Guide to Tasseography,* by Ravenna De Rhoswyn.

She placed each one on the table. Roisin leaned over, inspecting.

"Ah. A bit of magic."

"It's a new bit of magic to me," Daisy said. "But I would be willing to read for you."

Roisin nodded. "Very well. If the reading is suitable, then your wish is granted. Each girl will be able to wait until the night of her twenty-fifth birthday. And then, they must come to this barrow and claim their gifts. If—" The queen leaned forward, her green eyes glinting like the edge of a dagger's blade. "If the reading bodes well for that outcome."

Daisy's stomach churned. She thought she might be sick, but now hardly seemed like the time to nibble on a whole-wheat cracker.

The hobgoblin returned with a teapot. Daisy spooned the tea leaves into the cup, as Lily had done earlier that day at the shop. She poured the hot water over the waiting leaves, watching the mixture steep, darkening, her daughter's future tied up in how the leaves landed, in what she was able to discern from their patterns.

This was a terrible idea. Maybe Lily's worst.

What had Daisy been thinking? She was supposed to be the sensible one, after all.

The queen took up the teacup, its delicate shape and Victorian-esque pattern seeming out of place in her warrioress hands. She sipped, growing quiet.

Rhett leaned toward Daisy, brushing her hair away from her ear. His breath tickled her ear lobe as he whispered, "I feel magic. Feel it."

Daisy closed her eyes. She didn't have faerie magic in her veins like Rhett did. She was merely the daughter of two hippies who'd inherited a quirky old farmhouse from a mysterious relative.

Nothing magical about that.

Eccentric? Yeah. Magical? Not so much.

But Daisy's child? She would have faerie magic. It was guaranteed, a fate written in the stars long ago. Rhett had faerie magic in his blood. So, then, would their children.

Daisy placed her hand on her stomach. If her daughter had that magic, perhaps Daisy could harness it somehow?

Because Daisy didn't think she could do this tea-leaf reading without it. Not for a faerie queen who was also a seer.

The queen finished her tea and, with the fluid motion of one familiar with the process, turned the cup upside-down on the saucer.

Seconds ticked by. Tingles erupted on Daisy's skin.

Tingles. That was it, wasn't it?

The tiniest flicker of magic.

With a sudden flare of boldness, Daisy flipped over the cup.

At first, like before, the placement of the tea leaves seemed random, a bit of mess meant for the rubbish bin. But then, her vision changed. They assumed shapes.

Unlike in Lily's reading earlier that day, the leaves seemed to move, realigning themselves.

A bit of music seemed to whisper, a soft chant from the ether, the teacup quivering in a sparkling sea of blue magic.

The leaves floated up, becoming more than just shapes then. They whispered a story to her amid the soundtrack of that music.

Daisy knew, then, it was time to speak. She didn't know what she would say, but that the words would pour out when she began.

"Four Daughters of the Fae, destined to restore the balance. Light and Shadow must realign. They need each other. They exist in all of us. The Daughters will be gifted, as the queens of the tarot...

"One, practical and proud, hands in the earth, always a coin in her pocket...

"Another, fierce and bold, a forger of paths, a remover of obstacles...

"Another, a quiet, gentle soul, empath, friend to all creatures, her soft voice a healing balm...

"And the fourth, a twinkle in her eye, always mirth, always mischief, but secretly as fierce as the second...

"And the queen may reign. A woman of roses and thorns will emerge...

"So mote it be."

The energy left Daisy's body in a quick whoosh, the inside of the tent tilting sideways.

Rhett caught her.

She wrinkled her nose.

"Did I just swoon?" she asked.

He chuckled, adjusting his arms to cradle her better. "Afraid so."

"Ugh."

Rhett helped Daisy stand, and they faced the queen.

Roisin smirked. "Rhett and Daisy Fairshadow, your request is granted. On their twenty-fifth birthdays, I will meet each girl. But remember: until then, the unseelie fae hold unfettered sway over Foster Springs. You are the guardians of the forests until then.

"And tell Lily and Neer...when they're ready, I'll be waiting. I won't send for them, but there will come a time when they will follow the doe through the forest and, on a night of fireflies, seek my aid."

The air glittered around them, now filled with a buzzing, shimmering energy.

She and Rhett clung to each other as the spell swept over them.

When it passed, the queen and the barrow were gone. They stood in a moonlit forest, on a chilly autumn night, under a twinkle of cold, distant stars.

Rhett slid his arms around Daisy's waist.

She gazed up at him—this man, with his blond hair in its ponytail, those eyes often serious, but with a hidden bit of mirth for those who knew how to stir it.

"You are truly the most clever, most stubborn woman I've ever known," he growled.

Before she could respond, he covered her lips in a heated kiss.

She moaned, obliging him.

She slid her hands under his sweater, hands roaming as her lips parted to his.

Her knees almost buckled when his hands slid lower, drawing her against him.

What more could she do?

The midnight path had shown them the way. They'd entered the realm of the fae and returned.

The cold of the air seemed to fall away in the heat of the moment. Even the fae were forgotten as they explored one another.

And the rest?

Only the moon, only the stars, only the trees and the two lovers knew.

And none of them were telling.

The Cursed Woods

Faerie Spells: Book 4

"There is another world, but it is in this one."

———— ⟨∞⟩ ————

—William Butler Yeats

Chapter One

L ily leaned lightly against the wall, exhaling ever-so-slowly. Asleep. Her four-year-old daughter, Hazel, was finally, finally asleep.

A smile slid across Lily's face as she crept downstairs, where her drop-dead gorgeous fae husband waited.

"Neer," she whispered to her husband as she crept down the stairs to their farmhouse, avoiding the creakiest of steps.

Hazel had thoroughly enjoyed an evening spent catching fireflies with her father, while Lily had done some twilight gardening.

"She's asleep," Lily announced, but before she could even so much as waggle her eyebrows suggestively at her husband, she saw it was no use.

He was fast asleep, stretched out across a well-worn armchair, his long legs resting on an ottoman, a too-small afghan draped haphazardly across his body.

Lily lifted her fingers to her lips at the picture of her sexy husband—who normally looked more warrior fae than exhausted dad—thoroughly worn-out by their precocious daughter.

Not wanting to disturb Neer, Lily crept into the kitchen. There were dishes stacked in the sink, cups of tea forgotten halfway through resting on chipped saucers, and bundles of herbs harvested from the property's gardens hanging from the exposed rafters.

Lily turned on the sink, filling it with hot water and lavender-scented dish soap, catching a glimpse of the moon's crescent out the window. It looked impossibly large tonight, its light more golden than silver, and at another time in her life, Lily would've viewed such a sight as an invitation to stand barefoot in the yard and dance in the moon's glow.

But though she was married to a house-elf who would always guard and protect his family, Lily never forgot one thing: the forests around their farmhouse were filled with dangerous fae.

It was best not to attract their attention.

Instead of heeding the siren song of moonlight on a cool summer night, Lily grabbed a washcloth and started scrubbing.

Washing dishes had always been her favorite chore—aside from pulling weeds in the garden—ever since she was a child. There was something meditative about it, and people rarely interrupted your thoughts when you were doing dishes.

She added another teacup to the bamboo drying rack, her thoughts straying to a new line of mythology-inspired tea blends she and Daisy were planning for their shop, Tea Thyme, now a thriving mainstay of downtown Foster Springs, Virginia.

"Mommy, look!" a small, excited voice interrupted her mental ingredient list for the Persephone Tea Blend.

"Hazel Marigold, you're supposed to be in bed," Lily said, preparing her sternest look as she dropped the soapy dishcloth in the water with a splat and spun around.

Her annoyance faded into something else as she saw what Hazel was calling her attention to.

Hazel held her palm outstretched. In the center of her hand spun a swirl of fireflies, each one like a tiny, living flame.

"Sweetie, you were supposed to let the fireflies go, remember?" Lily said, her brain foggy. It had been a *long* day.

"I did, I swear. I know they can't live in the jar. I was thinking about fireflies, how they're made of magic like daddy, and I made these," Hazel announced, her voice full of pride and wonder. And pure innocence.

"You made them?" Lily said.

"Yup," her daughter said with a proud nod. "I wished and wished, and when I opened my eyes, they were there." Hazel frowned at her. "What's wrong, Mommy?"

"Nothing. You're just...you're supposed to be in bed," Lily said, trying to collect herself. "Asleep," she said, her tone more firm.

"You don't like it," Hazel said—the kid missed *nothing*.

Lily knelt in front of her daughter. More fireflies appeared around Hazel, swirling around her body now, as if fueled by her emotions.

"I think it's amazing," Lily insisted. "You are a very special little girl."

They'd always known Hazel would have abilities. She was half-fae, after all.

But that didn't mean Lily was ready for the moment her daughter conjured fireflies in their kitchen.

"It's faerie magic," Hazel said. "Like Daddy has."

It was true. Neer was a house-elf—a type of fae born to protect and serve others. Hazel would've inherited some abilities from her father. But while Neer could conjure the occasional energy ball in order to protect someone, he couldn't conjure living creatures at will.

Fireflies began to appear, dancing around the rafters, little balls of flickering light hovering among the bundles of dried lavender and landing on the rims of a few unwashed teacups.

Her daughter—at four years old—could conjure fireflies out of thin air.

That was some high-level magic for anyone, let alone a half-fae, half-human preschooler.

Neer walked in, eyes still blurry from sleep. He glanced down at his daughter. "You, young lady, are supposed to be in bed."

But before he could indulgently swing her up into his arms and carry her back to bed, he glanced at the kitchen.

"What's this?" he said.

"Your daughter," Lily said, trying to sound cheerful for Hazel's sake, "has a gift."

THERE WERE ABOUT A hundred fireflies in his kitchen.

Neer met his wife's eyes, communicating with her in that wordless way they'd developed over the years.

Hazel did this? he asked with a raise of his eyebrows.

Mmhmm. Lily's pursed lips and half-nod said.

Neer pressed his lips together in a firm line, not sure how to respond.

They'd known Hazel would have some faerie magic. She was half-fae, after all. And there were hints that Lily had some long-sleeping magic of her own, and such things could be passed on from parent to child.

Neer was fae—had grown up in the faerie realm, had spent years serving witch families in the human world.

But nothing could've prepared him for the tiny, glittering creatures swirling in the kitchen of his farmhouse, or the look of concern on his daughter's face as she stood there, in her floral-print nightgown, waiting for his reaction.

This was important—he and Lily both knew that. They'd discussed many times how they should react if Hazel showed signs of magical abilities. Still, a late-night firefly invasion in their kitchen was far more than either of them could've prepared themselves for.

"You don't like it?" Hazel asked, her lips forming a pout.

"It's quite impressive, actually," Neer insisted. He scooped up his daughter. "But perhaps we should let them outside now. That's where they live. They'll be happiest out there, don't you think?"

Hazel wiggled in his arms. "I don't know how to do that, Daddy. I just started making magic like, five minutes ago."

A quick glance behind him assured him that fireflies were invading the living room too.

He needed to teach his daughter how to control her magic—and he needed to do it fast.

He swung Hazel down and gently set her on the floor. Neer knelt beside her. "The fireflies are beautiful, but remember what we said earlier? About how they belong outside?"

Her small face furrowed up in a serious look. "I remember. But I don't know how."

Fireflies danced around her tiny body, as if somehow knowing she was the source of the magic that brought them here. An unseen wind blew around her. Neer felt the magic within it, fierce and beautiful and wild.

Whatever magic his daughter possessed, it far surpassed his own.

And it would only grow as she aged.

"I bet you know how," he said, his voice gentle. "If you close your eyes, I bet somewhere inside, you have the ability to send the fireflies back to the fields and the forests, where they'll be happiest."

Hazel closed her eyes. The wind set her hair swirling, her nightgown billowing about her legs.

Neer shivered. Truthfully, he'd hoped they would have many years until her powers surfaced—if they ever did. Many half-fae, half-human children had magical abilities that remained dormant their entire lives.

Clearly, Hazel was not one of those children.

Hazel's eyes flew open. A big grin graced her lips. "I know! I've got it!" she said.

She raised her hands toward the ceiling. "Abracadabra!" she shouted.

Lightning flashed outside. Thunder rumbled. The wind in the kitchen grew into a roar. And more fireflies appeared, thousands of them inside the house.

Hazel's eyes grew wide. "Daddy, I think I made it worse."

Neer could only stare.

It was Lily, then, who swooped in. His wife, who he knew had always hoped their daughter would never possess such magic.

Amid the wild wind that sent the curtains flying and carefully tied bundles of dried herbs toppling from the rafters to the floor, the tablecloth now tangled amid the oaken chairs, Lily knelt before their daughter.

In her floral tank top and black leggings, she was so much of the human realm. But she'd learned how to walk the fine line between human and faerie, magical and mundane, with admirable grace.

"Mommy, I can't do it," Hazel said, panic in her voice now. The wind tore at her, and she looked so small, so scared.

Lily pulled Hazel into her lap, cradling her amid the storm.

Thunder clapped again. Fat drops of rain now pelted the farmhouse.

"What do we do when we feel stormy inside?" Lily said, her voice calm, like a lighthouse guiding a lost ship to shore.

"Let the rain fall down," she whispered to her daughter. "Let the storm blow past."

It was a trick Lily had taught their daughter for handling overwhelming emotions. When the storm inside grew too fierce, release the emotion, let it go, like the storm releasing the rain. Find calm and relax.

Let the rain fall down.

It worked for helping Hazel cope with small, everyday frustrations in her life.

Would it work for magic gone awry?

Hazel inhaled deeply, still cradled in her mother's arms. She sucked in a deep breath, and exhaled.

Once.

Twice.

Three times.

The wind died down.

The rain stopped.

And the sea of fireflies vanished, bit by bit, until all that remained was the aftermath of the magical storm.

Hazel snuggled into her mother's embraced. "It worked, Mommy!"

"Good job!" Lily said, planting a kiss on Hazel's forehead.

Neer leaned against the doorframe, watching his wife and daughter as they snuggled on the kitchen floor, surrounded by scattered tea towels and broken bits of dried herbs.

Then, he did the only thing he could think of.

He hugged them both.

Chapter Two

L ily stared at the debris in her kitchen, standing on trembling legs while holding Hazel.

Neer cleared his throat. "I guess we're going to need a broom," he said.

She sent him a look that said, *That's the understatement of the century*.

"Mommy, can I have some hot chocolate?" Hazel asked, squirming.

Lily set her daughter down. "No. It's..." she glanced at the cuckoo clock. "Quarter til eleven. Way past your bedtime. Way past Daddy's bedtime too," Lily said, remembering the sight of her sleeping husband.

She caught her husband barely suppressing a yawn as he grabbed a broom and dustpan from a closet.

"Daddy is going to tuck you in, okay, pumpkin?" Lily said.

"Can I have a glass of water first?" Hazel asked. "I'm thirsty."

"A small one."

Lily gave her daughter a kiss on the forehead while Neer filled a glass halfway with water. After she'd gulped it down, he offered Hazel a piggyback ride to bed, giving Lily a look that assured her they would talk later.

The sound of Hazel peppering her father with questions as they made their way through the living room and up the stairs meant that it would take at least three bedtime stories to get her to sleep.

Lily grabbed the broom, but she couldn't sweep. She could only stare into the now eerily silent kitchen. There were bits of dried herbs everywhere—she always hung as much of her harvest as possible in the rafters to dry, and bits of everything from yarrow to lavender to blackberry leaves now littered the room.

It wasn't the loss of the herbs. They had plenty of harvest time left this year, and their gardens were always bountiful.

No. It was the idea that her young daughter could work such powerful magic out of the blue.

And surely her powers would only grow.

She was supposed to go to preschool in the fall, and then start kindergarten the following year. What if she conjured fireflies in the classroom or a snowstorm on the playground?

Lily had never been overly obsessed with normalcy. She'd been raised by eccentric parents, and her childhood in upstate New York had been full of love, nature, and adventure. Her father, a professor by trade, had taught his daughters about nature in a way that blended beauty and wonder, and her mother, a hippie with a flair for jewelry-making and singing, had taught her daughters to embrace their unique gifts and follow their intuition.

Was it any surprise then, when Lily and her sister, Daisy, had inherited this old farmhouse and the accompanying tea business from their Great-Aunt Marigold, they'd jumped on the opportunity?

It had worked out. Daisy had married to the town's most eligible—and reclusive—bachelor, Rhett Fairshadow. The two had three daughters now: five-year-old Mel, short for Camelia, and three-year-old twins, Calendula, or Callie, and Periwinkle, whom they all called Peri.

It had been almost six years since Daisy and Rhett had braved the forest to meet the faerie queen, Queen Roisin. Lily remembered pacing the floors of Fairshadow Manor, Neer grumbling at her to sit down, as they waited for her sister and brother-in-law to return.

That night they'd learned the girls were destined to grow up to be entwined in a faerie war that simmered in the forests of Foster Springs, one between the seelie and unseelie fae. Seelie versus unseelie: light against shadow. The fae who granted wishes versus those who bestowed curses.

Lily replayed their conversation that night, watching it like a movie in her mind, her heart pounding, blood roaring in her ears.

The sound of the broom clattering to the floor broke her out of the memory.

Rhett's family had a centuries-long connection to the fae of Foster Springs. That's why Roisin had chosen his daughters to bestow the necklaces upon—on their twenty-fifth birthdays.

But she'd never explained how Lily's daughter would be involved. Lily had spent many a sleepless night when she was pregnant and then when Hazel was a newborn, furtively glancing out windows into the night, jumping at sudden sounds, waiting for a message that it was their turn to visit the queen. Surely Queen Roisin would have some details to deliver about their daughter, right?

But she hadn't, in all these years, summoned Lily and Neer. Lily had started to assume the news of the prophecy had been delivered via Daisy, and that was that. It didn't make her less anxious about Hazel's destiny, but it meant they had some time to figure things out.

The sound of a cell phone vibrating sent Lily jumping, hand flying to her throat.

With an unspoken curse, she grabbed her phone off the kitchen island. Seeing her sister's name, she answered.

"Hey."

"Hey," Daisy said, but there was concern in that single word.

"What's wrong?" Lily asked. "Are the girls okay?" For all she knew, they'd all started displaying powers at once.

"They're fine. But I thought you should know..." Daisy trailed off, as if she didn't want to be the bearer of bad news.

"If it's faerie news, just say it," Lily said. A headache began to form, a tight band squeezing her head and causing her temples to pound.

She needed a good night's rest. Something told her she wasn't going to get one.

Over the phone, she heard Daisy sigh. "The fae are really stirring tonight. It feels...off. Unusual somehow. I wanted to warn you, just to be on the safe side."

Daisy and Rhett's house, Fairshadow Manor, was surrounded by forests where the unseelie fae gathered most often. Over the years, they'd all come to suspect that the unseelie king's barrow was somewhere on the sprawling acreage of the estate, but they had no way of knowing for sure.

"Thanks for letting us know," Lily said. She went into the living room and flopped onto the overstuffed sofa, drawing a vibrant pink crocheted throw pillow into her lap. "It's been a weird night here."

"Oh no," Daisy said. "Like, magically weird?"

Lily didn't ask how Daisy knew. Probably the edge in Lily's voice. Though Lily loved to dabble in spells, tea-leaf reading, and other forms of witchcraft, she wasn't big on fae magic.

The irony that she'd fallen hard and fast for a house-elf who was one-hundred percent fae didn't escape her. She loved Neer, and he'd taught her that faerie magic wasn't all bad.

But still, sometimes it was a lot. Lily's first encounter with the fae had ended with a curse that sent her into Sleeping Beauty land for a couple months—until Daisy had found a way to end that curse.

"Yeah, definitely weirdness of the magical variety," Lily confirmed. She leaned back, tucking her legs underneath her, cradling the pillow while she recounted the events of the evening.

"What does Neer have to say about all of this?" Daisy asked after Lily finished telling the tale.

"I don't know yet. We haven't had a chance to talk. He's trying to get Hazel back to sleep."

"But it's early, right? I thought you suspected she'd be in her early teens before she manifested any kind of abilities?" Daisy said.

It was Lily's turn to sigh. "We did. Everything Neer could gather in the faerie realm suggested that whatever abilities she had would appear later."

"Hmm," Daisy said. Lily imagined her sister pacing in her kitchen, spooning loose-leaf tea into a strainer and powering on the electric kettle. "You know what's weird? You know what Queen Roisin said to us that night?"

Lily retraced every memory she had of their conversation that night years ago. "I remember the prophecy. Besides that? No."

"She said you and Neer would seek her out. On a night when fireflies danced."

Lily leaned forward, the throw pillow tumbling out of her lap and onto the floor.

"What?" She cringed, hoping the exclamation hadn't disturbed Hazel.

Her blood roared in her ears. In the distance, she heard Daisy apologizing, saying she should've said something sooner.

But it didn't matter. She knew why Daisy hadn't told her. Because Lily would've agonized over that piece of information until it tore her apart. Best not say anything until it was time, right?

"I'm not mad," Lily assured her sister. "I get it."

Silent greeted her, stretching. It was the kind of silence she'd come to anticipate when Daisy was preparing to say something she'd rather not say.

"There's a doe who will guide you to Queen Roisin's barrow. Somehow, I think she'll know—the doe, that is. But Queen Roisin too. They'll both be waiting for you, like they were for me and Rhett that night."

"It worked out for you guys, though," Lily said, heart hammering. Her vision tunneled. She rose and grabbed a tin of calming blend of essential oils from a nearby drawer, smoothing chamomile, hyssop, and lavender scented coconut oil onto her wrists and inhaling deeply.

"Yes. It did. It's been over five years, and we haven't heard from her since. And Queen Roisin, she's strong, powerful, but also fair. I wouldn't cross her, but I think...in her own way, the queen needs us. I don't doubt that her motives are a bit self-serving, even if she is seelie fae, but I think she's looking for...how should I put this?"

"Basically, she's looking out for herself, but she doesn't mind doing something that benefits us if it benefits her as well?" Lily chimed in.

Daisy chuckled. "Yeah. Sorry. I'm exhausted. It's way past my bedtime."

Lily inhaled the scent of lavender, grounding herself. She imagined roots stretching from her feet into the waiting earth, strong and nurturing.

Neer came downstairs and gave her a nod that indicated Hazel was asleep again.

"Daisy, I know it's past your bedtime, but is there any way you could come over tonight?"

"Of course. Let me get dressed and throw a few things to-gether, and I'll be there," Daisy said. "Does this mean...?"

Lily glanced at Neer, who was cocking an eyebrow in the way he always did when he knew something was up between the sisters.

"I don't know yet," Lily said. "I'll share what you told me with Neer, and we'll go from there."

Something told her that her house-elf husband wasn't go-ing to like a late-night journey to the seelie queen's barrow.

Something else told her that they might not have a choice.

She looked at Neer, who had his arms crossed over his chest, gaze fixed on her.

I'm waiting, his expression said.

Lily ended the phone call with Daisy, and then turned to her husband.

"Maybe you should sit down," Lily said.

NEER SHUT THE BACK door and stepped out into the night. Crickets chirped, and an owl hooted in the distance. He strode to the edge of the forest, amid the high grasses beyond which lay the tall reaches of the trees.

There, he knelt and placed his palms against the earth. Tingles of energy erupted along his skin, his hair dancing in the static electricity of his magic. Green currents of magic reached down into the earth like a root's tendrils, exploring.

The layers of protective magic he'd placed around the house and gardens held.

He released the magic with a sigh, staring out into the night.

The faerie queen.

That was not what he wanted tonight. Or any night, for that matter. What he wanted was a second slice of strawberry-rhubarb pie, and a night that ended with him snuggling up against his wife.

He groaned inwardly. Married life was making him soft.

It happened, he'd been warned. Not so much because of marriage, but because, when a house-elf was matched with a family or charge who wasn't magical by nature, their own magical nature grew quieter to match. It was the nature of a house-elf's magic, something that allowed them to blend better into the family they protected, assuring harmony between the guardian and the ones he'd guarded.

He'd fallen in love with Lily—her strength, her ability to face her fears, and her mix of playfulness and wisdom. Her imagination never ceased to amaze him, and she'd proven herself more courageous than many fae he knew, let alone most humans.

He didn't want to leave his family this night, certainly not to go to the seelie queen's barrow.

To do what, exactly? To say what? To request what?

Lily didn't know. Neither did he.

But he was a house-elf, a faerie to his core.

And the fae did not question prophecy. Roisin was a seer, after all, as well as a queen. If she said they would come to her barrow this night, they would.

There was no other choice. They would go.

"Neer?"

He turned at the sound of his wife's voice. Her tone was worried.

He walked over to her and wrapped his arms around her. "I wanted to check the wards before we left," he said.

She snuggled into his embrace. "Good thinking."

"They're holding well," he assured her.

He'd spent years perfecting the series of mystically charged barriers around their home. It had been tricky—they couldn't keep out all fae, only the unseelie, or Neer himself couldn't enter the home. And the protective barriers couldn't be something that normal, non-magical humans would notice, so they had to be both unseen and unfelt.

A difficult feat, but he'd managed.

The sound of tires crunching on gravel interrupted their midnight embrace.

Lily drew away. "Daisy's here."

She glanced down. "I guess I better change into something more befitting meeting fae royalty," she said with an exaggerated flourish of her hands.

In the night, though, his fae vision caught the nervous blush that flared in her cheeks, the shiver that wracked her body that had nothing to do with the cool night air. She was nervous—afraid, even.

They walked back to the house, and Lily stepped through the back door to the house, while Neer circled around to meet Daisy. He tugged the tote bag from her arms and wrapped her in a hug.

"Thanks for coming," he said.

"No problem," Daisy said. She glanced up at him, wrinkling her nose. "Are you wearing human clothes to meet Queen Roisin? Or going full-on fae ensemble?"

She laughed—no doubt at the scowl now plastered on his face.

"You and your sister," he said with a groan. "Are of one mind."

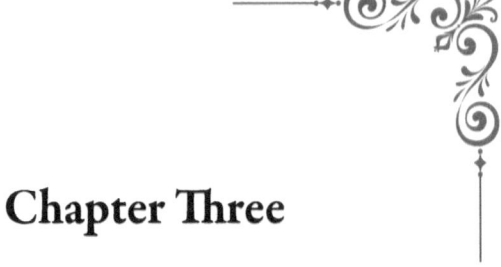

Chapter Three

For about the thousandth time, Lily smoothed her dress. It was a turquoise maxi dress, one she'd found at a local thrift store. She'd added a couple of wooden bracelets, a pair of smoky quartz earrings, and a point of green fluorite on a long, silver chain.

Neer stood beside her at the edge of Fairshadow Forest. With some prodding from Daisy, he'd donned a pair of black britches and a midnight-blue tunic, his faerie key glistening on a leather cord around his neck.

Lily clasped his hand before releasing how sweaty her palms were. She withdrew hers and wiped both of her hands against her dress.

"Do you think the doe Daisy talked about just shows up, or do we need to summon it?" Lily asked.

Neer's sharp gaze was fixed on the forest in front of them. In the background, Lily heard the sounds of fae howling, chanting, and the strains of discordant music. Her heart hammered, but she tried to block it out.

Yeah, Daisy was right. The unseelie fae were especially wild tonight—as if they knew.

Lily shivered, though the air wasn't cold, merely pleasantly cool against her skin.

Normally, entering Fairshadow Forest at night was usually a recipe for disaster, but Rhett and Neer both theorized that the doe would lead them safely through the forests. Her magic, the theory went, was powerful enough that not even the unseelie would come near them.

Lily had a different theory—that the doe was a sacred creature, a being of both nature and magic that even the unseelie respected.

They had no idea which of these theories was true, but it didn't matter.

Bottom line? Do not enter the forest until the doe appeared.

"It feels like it's been an hour," Lily said.

"It's been ten minutes," Neer said.

"Which is basically an hour when we're this close to the unseelie fae," she countered, shivering again.

"What do you suggest?" Neer asked.

"I don't think she's going to just appear. I think we have to, you know, ask or beseech or whatever."

"Beseech?" She heard the quirked eyebrow in his voice.

"You know what I mean," Lily said.

"Are you suggesting a summoning spell?"

"I mean, a spell seems a bit much," she said. "Maybe more of a magical SOS."

"Hmm." In the darkness, she could almost hear the gears turning in Neer's mind.

Lily's attempts at spell-casting, limited as they were over the years, hadn't gone great. Although one of those spells had introduced her to the love of her life, so there was that. These days, she stuck to reading tea leaves at the shop and dabbling in tarot on full-moon nights.

"There might be a way. Magic calling to magic," he mused. She could hear the wonder in his voice. For a long time, Neer had shunned his house-elf magic. But over the years, he'd found healing, and with that healing had come a sense of joy.

She could see that, whatever the future held, he would enjoy teaching Hazel about magic, about her gifts, about the best parts of faerie lore. Even when he read her fairy tales, she heard the joy in his voice, the way he interlaced human stories with bits of faerie wisdom.

Lily reached out and touched his shoulder, leaning up to kiss his cheek. "Call her," she whispered. "Magic to magic."

He nodded. "Let's sit," he said.

They sat cross-legged in the grass, hands palms up on their thighs, knees touching. She's come to love the feel of Neer's magic, a wonderful blend of cool rain and wild earth, a scent of ferns and pine, with just a touch of bonfire's crackle in it.

He reached out and clasped her hands.

She followed the pattern of his breathing—deep breath in, slow exhale. Repeat.

With each breath, Lily's body seemed to sink more deeply into the earth, as if the roots themselves were caressing her skin. At the same time, the stars in the sky seemed to sigh and lean in, eager for a taste of the magic.

It had been so long since they'd worked magic together. Lily had forgotten the physicality of it, the sensuality of magic singing along her skin.

Her hands still in Neer's, Lily's eyes flickered open.

A bit of heat lightning danced in the sky above. In its light, she caught the half-quirk of a smile on Neer's lips.

"Is it done?" she asked, rather breathless.

His thumbs traced her hands. "It is."

In a shimmer of blue and silvery magic, the doe appeared. Her fur was white, just as Daisy had described her. Lily and Neer rose, neither of them daring to say a word.

Wisps of deep blue magic danced around the doe. She turned and walked into the woods, not stopping to look back.

They both understood. Lily didn't even have to glance at her husband to know.

Hand in hand, they followed.

NEER SWALLOWED HARD as the door to the seelie queen's barrow appeared in the hillside. Royal blue, like the brightest of sapphires, it beckoned.

The doe vanished. He released Lily's hand.

"Don't be nervous," Lily whispered in the hush of the forest. "You're seelie fae too, after all." The words sounded like they were spoken as much for her own benefit as for his, though.

He nodded. Of course, Neer knew they had nothing to fear from Queen Roisin. He wasn't one of her subjects, technically—though house-elves were seelie, or light fae, they were generally considered bond to the magical families they served rather than the fae courts.

But what would the queen ask of them? It had to be something. They wouldn't get anything, not even advice, for nothing.

The door creaked open. Lily stepped forward and peered inside, then reached her hand into the pool of swirling magicks.

"Ready?" she asked, and he heard the hint of joy in that single word. Lily could be fearful of the fae, but she also loved a good, old-fashioned adventure.

He guessed that was where Hazel got it from.

"Yes. I don't want to leave Hazel any longer than we need to tonight," he said.

He followed Lily through the doorway, magic tingling along his skin.

Neer sucked in a breath as they emerged in Queen Roisin's barrow. Roisin was a faerie of summer and abundance, after all, and there was no shortage of flowers in her demesne.

Lily covered a grin with her hand, her eyes wide with delight as she gazed around. A natural-born gardener and trained herbalist, she no doubt felt she was in paradise.

"This is the most amazing place I've ever seen," she exclaimed, spinning around to study roses the size of dinner plates, ferns up to their shoulders, and countless other varieties of flora.

"I'm glad you like it, Lily McAllister," a woman's voice said.

From between two twisting oaks covered in dangling dark-green ivy, Queen Roisin emerged. Her long, auburn hair hung in two plaits, one draped over each shoulder. She wore a gown of emerald green, fastened with a simple gold belt. Tattoos of thorny vines snaked up her arms.

Neer kneeled. He couldn't help it. Because, regardless of what she wore, this faerie woman exuded power. It swept over him like a gust, a reminder that she was ancient and far more powerful than almost anyone who crossed her path.

Lily glanced at Neer and back at Queen Roisin, as if uncertain if she should bow too. She seemed to hesitate before attempting an awkward curtsey.

The queen studied both of them as if she couldn't decide whether to be amused or exasperated.

After a moment, a young, mousy woman with pointed ears and wide blue eyes appeared behind the queen.

"Neer of the house-elves," Roisin said, clearing her throat. "Rise, please, and take a walk with me." Roisin turned to the young fae woman behind her and said, "Arielle, please show Lily to my throne chambers. I'll join you shortly."

Lily shot a nervous glance at him. *Don't leave me alone in this place*, her eyes said.

You'll be fine, he told her in that mind-speak they'd perfected over the years.

"This way, miss," the young woman, Arielle, said. Her hair was as blue as her eyes, a choppy cut offsetting high cheekbones and lips stained the color of a ripe cherry. She wore a simple lilac-hued gown that skimmed her knees and a bit of blue crystal about her throat.

If Neer had to guess, Arielle's station was somewhere between servant and student. Whatever her place in Roisin's court, the blue magic that danced in wisps around her assured him she was no ordinary handmaiden.

To her credit, Lily followed Arielle down a path canopied with vines that grew over a pergola, amid glittering fairy lights. He watched them go, his gut tightening with every step Lily took further from him in this strange, underground realm.

Neer turned to Roisin. What audience could she want with him and him alone? He didn't wish to pledge fealty to a faerie court—such deals rarely led to anything but disaster.

The seelie queen's barrow was a labyrinth of sorts, like an underground forest of interconnected paths that someone could spend the rest of their life learning how to navigate. After more than two centuries captive in the barrow—part of a peace treaty of sorts with the unseelie king, Oberon—Queen Roisin navigated the space with familiar ease.

She led him to a part of the barrow where will-o-the-wisps glittered in the impossibly tall and thick branches of gnarled oaks and wide ashes, glistening green moss clinging to the bases of the trees while ivy dangled here and there.

It was beautiful, but there was a darkness in the space beneath the aged trees, one that sent a shiver down his spine.

Roisin pointed to a bench that appeared carved of a single piece of wood and then polished to a shine.

"Sit, please."

Shadows danced around them in the flickering light of the will-o-the-wisps, the tiny fae creatures like living lanterns in the queen's barrow.

Neer slid into the bench. Roisin, however did not. Instead, she paced.

"It's interesting to me that you've been here, in this territory, for so many years and yet only now do we meet."

Uh-oh. He needed to tread carefully—not just for himself, but for Lily and Hazel, as well. "I didn't want to intrude, my lady."

She had turned away from him, her hands clasped behind her back. She spun slowly to face him, her intense gaze locking with his. "I don't ask for oath or bond, Neer of the house-elves. Your sacred duty is to the family you are called to serve, first and foremost. I respect that of your kind."

He exhaled.

"What, then, do you ask of me?" The words sprang from his tongue before he could stop then.

"Do you journey?"

"You mean...what? Astral projection? No, your majesty."

"The journey of visions. I need you to understand the curse, and how what is came to be. You will teach them, the daughters of the prophecy and the queens whose powers slumber yet."

His daughter. She meant Hazel and her cousins.

Roisin strode across the grove and grasped his chin. "Will you follow willingly, house-elf? To see what was? Then, you might teach them to understand what now is and what is yet to come. What they will be."

Her fingernails cut into his chin, her grip forceful but not painfully so.

What choice did he have? He'd come this far.

"Yes, my lady. I will."

Chapter Four

L ily couldn't help but pace.

Queen Roisin's barrow was a far cry from the terrifying labyrinth of nightmares Lily had been trapped in all those years ago. Though they were underground, the air felt cool and breezy, and everything seemed to sparkle in golden light reminiscent of sunshine.

The sheer quantity of flowers put Lily a bit more at ease, but here, alone with a strange fae woman, her stomach churned.

Arielle studied her, a slight smirk playing at her lips. Away from the queen, Arielle seemed more sure of herself, a bit mischievous, even.

Lily was *not* certain she liked that. Mischievous fae could still be dangerous, after all.

"I assure you, I'm not your enemy," Arielle said, as if reading Lily's thoughts.

Lily jumped back. Was she reading her thoughts?

"If you were, would you come right out and say it?" Lily asked, trying to keep her tone light.

The throne chambers was really more of a throne tent, an intricately carved throne chair on a dais surrounded by opulent cushions and high-backed chairs, candles flickering in silver candelabra, vines climbing the wooden pillars that held up the tent's heavy canvas fabric.

Arielle quirked an eyebrow. "I'm fae. I can't lie." The concern in her words seemed genuine, as if she were both mortified and mystified to be accused of such a thing.

Lily forced herself to stop pacing, stopping instead to study the fae woman. She'd once considered herself a good judge of character and of situations in general. The troll attack had changed that, but the intervening years had brought with them some of her old faith in herself.

Arielle seemed young. If she'd been human, no older than twenty or so, though with the fae, appearances could be deceiving. But there was something youthful in her mannerisms—a sense of mischief, a dash of overconfidence, but underneath it all, a shyness she desperately wanted to keep hidden.

Lily sighed, knots of tension in her loosening a bit. "How do you know Queen Roisin?"

"I'm her ward."

"Ward? I'm not familiar with the expression."

A flicker of sadness moved across the young woman's face, like a swift-moving cloud casting shadows over the sun-drenched fields. "My parents...were killed. They left the barrow to get a healing plant we couldn't find here. Unseelie fae found them. My father returned with the plant before succumbing to his wounds. My mother never returned."

Her face fell. She sniffed, then shook her head and held it high. "Queen Roisin made a promise to my father before he passed that she would raise me, see that I was trained in all manner of faerie magicks. She says I'll play a great role one day in what is to come."

Lily shivered. *What is to come.* That meant a battle between seelie fae and unseelie. And Lily's daughter and nieces would be right in the middle of it.

"They might be a while. I believe they're vision journeying," Arielle said. She went to a nearby table and poured a cup of tea from a silver teapot. She stirred a bit of honey and cream into it and handed it to Lily, then poured herself another. "We should sit."

Lily wrapped her hands around the cup, inhaling a scent slightly earthy with a bit of fruitiness.

She sat in the corner of the room on a floor cushion across from Arielle and sipped her tea, grateful for such a familiar ritual in such an unfamiliar place. "Mmm. Hawthorn berries and mugwort," she said, savoring the flavor.

"Yes," Arielle said, looking at her over the rim of her teacup. "Queen Roisin tells me you are a healer and teamaker."

Lily smiled. "You left out gardener," she said with a half-laugh.

"Gardener," Arielle said, a bit of wonder in her voice. "When the seelie can live under the stars again, I'll have a garden. A small cottage with a garden, and I'll pull weeds under the stars, bathed in the light of the moon."

"That sounds magical," Lily said. "But you can't have gardens here?"

Arielle shrugged. "We can have many things here. But I'm focused on my training now."

Lily sipped her tea, her body relaxing into the cushion beneath her. Arielle's voice seemed softer, more lilting, almost like music.

"What are your powers?" Lily asked. She went to take another sip of her tea, and frowned. The cup was empty.

Arielle reached out and took the cup from Lily's hands.

"I'm a seer, but not of the future. Not like the queen. I see within—deep within. What is hidden beneath the layers within us."

Arielle set Lily's cup on a nearby table. "My power is not to see the future," she continued, her voice growing deep, seeming to reverberate with magic. "My power is to reveal what is within."

Lily frowned, her heart racing. Too late, she remembered the warning: *do not eat or drink anything in the faerie realm.*

"What did you do to me?" she demanded.

Arielle shook her head. "I didn't harm you. I didn't curse you. I didn't poison you. The tea is a spell, that's all. At the queen's request. To help you to find, to see the magic within."

The magic within? Curse the fae and their riddles.

"Within what?" Lily asked.

Arielle cocked her head, as if the need for clarification were ridiculous. "Within yourself, of course."

NEER FELT THE MOMENT the waking world drifted away. His body grew lighter, swaying, and then a swirl of iridescent shadows carried him to another time, another place.

This was far, far beyond any magic he possessed. It was all Queen Roisin, the magic of a faerie seer who had long ago mastered her abilities.

The shadows grew more intense, until only inky blackness surrounded them.

A scent filled his nostrils—something acrid mixed with smoke. And there was another stench, too, dark and cloying, like decay mixed with the heavy scent of pollen.

And death.

The shadows faded, and he and Roisin stood in a forest filled with patchy fog. Bodies littered the ground. They were fae. Wisps of magic in various colors filled the air, remnants of a battle waged.

The battle was over. The bodies shimmered, their auras of magic now visible, and then they faded to dust, leaving only the scents of the forest in their wake.

"Why would you bring me here?" he asked, turning away from the scene. The day was cloudy and gray, a cold spring day before the buds had opened on the trees, and the sun fought to break through the clouds.

"I need you to see. What's at stake. Because on this day, the day after my father was murdered by King Oberon and the unseelie, I made a deal." She gave a sad, bitter snort. "Foolish, I know. A faerie queen making a faerie deal. But I was deep in my grief, and new to the throne. I wanted to save the lives of the seelie fae, but the unseelie fae too. I thought it was worth it then."

Her eyes glistened with unshed tears, and he saw now what a burden she bore. She was a warrior who'd made a deal that wouldn't allow her to fight, not even if her people needed her to. She turned to him and took his hand.

"I had a vision long ago. And that vision has given me hope for centuries. When you arrived in Foster Springs, I felt your magic. And I knew it would soon be time."

"Time for what? How does this involve my daughter?"

"Hazel is gifted not once, not twice, but three times. First, by your house-elf magic. Second, by the magic that sleeps inside her mother's veins, ready to be awoken. And third, by the magic of Foster Springs, of these forests, of this land.

"But her magic has awoken too soon. I want you to see what's at stake. When I made the deal with Oberon, I thought I was saving everyone—my people. His. The humans of Foster Springs. The forests themselves. But I was wrong. I cursed us all. The woods of Foster Springs are Oberon's, and he grows more arrogant, more cruel with each passing year."

Neer nodded. She was right, of course. The unseelie grew bolder as the years passed. How long until the humans were no longer safe?

"I bound myself with that deal. But your daughter and her cousins, they will not be bound. They are the greatest hope for the seelie fae and for the humans of Foster Springs."

The scene fell away amid swirls of shadows.

When Neer blinked, he and Queen Roisin sat once more in the grove of ancient, mossy trees in her barrow.

She leaned forward. "Hazel's magic is so powerful. It has awoken far too soon. She's not safe. The unseelie fae are drawn to it."

Neer jumped up, his heart racing. "She's in danger?"

Roisin nodded. "King Oberon senses her magic. He will send a changeling to take her place. If you and Lily combine your magicks, you can stop him. You can bind Hazel's magic so that it sleeps. She'll forget this night, like a dream that fades upon waking. And then, someday, when she's ready, Hazel can come to me, and claim her amulet. Her magic will reawaken then."

Neer's head spun. It was a lot to process. They'd suspected as much, but to hear the queen say it...that was a different matter entirely.

"I need to find Lily," he said, starting to pace. "We need to get home to our daughter."

Roisin placed a hand on his arm. "You will. I can transport you both to your daughter's side in an instant. But Lily has a journey of her own to walk before she's ready."

"Is my daughter safe?" The queen was a seer. Surely she could tell.

Roisin raised her head skyward and closed her eyes. After a few seconds that felt like an eternity, she opened them.

"For now."

There was a darkness lurking in those two simple words that Neer didn't care for at all.

Chapter Five

The heaviness in Lily's veins changed, pulsing with a sort of restless energy.

"Follow me," Arielle said, offering a long, slender hand. Lily took it, and Arielle helped her to her feet.

They left the tent and walked down a path lined with tall, gnarled trees draped in moss and vines. Tiny will-o-the-wisps danced everywhere, reminiscent of the fireflies that Hazel had conjured earlier that night.

They entered a clear space, the only thing above them the impossibly high ceiling of the barrow, where vines and moss tangled with large gemstone points.

"Stand here," Arielle said, positioning Lily in the center of the large, open space. It felt almost like an underground magical practice arena, the ground beneath her a pattern of flagstone broken only by gemstone mosaics.

Arielle stepped away, backing up and giving Lily a wide berth.

Why? Was she going to explode?

As if sensing the question, Arielle smirked. "Don't worry. It's just that, when latent magic is awoken after so many years dormant, it can be unpredictable. It won't hurt you. But I'd rather not take a blast of what I'm sensing is some rather powerful magic."

Lily snorted. Yeah, right. Aside from dabbling in reading tea leaves and tarot cards, and her longstanding love affair with gardening and herbalism, Lily had always doubted she had much, if any, magical ability.

Still, years ago, Neer's mentor turned nemesis had taunted her with the knowledge that she had some sort of dormant magic.

And now, Arielle's promise to awaken it. At the behest of the faerie queen. No, there had to be something.

Lily had to admit that she was intrigued. Would she be psychic? Predicting the future would be fun *and* useful, although reading people's thoughts sounded terrifying.

Wait. What if she didn't want to know the future? What if she saw something she couldn't unsee?

Telekinesis, then? That could be interesting.

"Ready?" Arielle asked, snapping Lily out of her musings.

"As I'll ever be," Lily said, shaking her body out. Tingles had erupted all over her skin, like the air was charged with energy.

"Close your eyes and think back to the first time you remember using magic—even the smallest trace of it," Arielle instructed—from a safe distance, of course.

Lily racked her brain, trying to remember. Truthfully, she'd always been fascinated by magic. Her favorite books had always featured witches as main characters, and she'd devoured every paranormal and supernatural show in existence.

She remembered making her own "book of shadows" out of construction paper as a kid, after she'd read that witches kept them. She'd used green paper for anything to do with plants and herbs, red for love spells, and blue for anything to do with the moon or stars.

Lily closed her eyes, recalling the slightly rough feel of the paper beneath her fingers, the squeak of the marker as she wrote a list of herbs and their magical properties.

It was in their childhood bedroom, in that old Victorian house they grew up in, the room she shared with Daisy. She remembered the rainy October day, the gray skies outside the wide windows. Daisy sat on a cushioned window seat, surrounded by stuffed animals and floral print throw pillows, reading a Nancy Drew mystery.

Her sister—younger by eighteen months, but you'd never know it—had cast her a dirty look. "Can you do that *quietly*, please? I'm almost at the good part."

"I'm. Almost. Done," Lily said, copying the last herb and its meaning from one of their mom's assorted new-age texts.

With a smile, she closed the book, allowing her hand to come to rest on the cover, made of dark blue paper on which she'd written *Lily McAllister's Book of Shadows.* Surrounding the curvy script were lightning bolts and stars drawn with a glitter pen.

Lily smiled. Just like a real witch.

Her smile turned to a frown as she realized. She was *not* a witch. Real witches had powers. Lily had none.

Lily tucked the book into a drawer. That night, after her sister had fallen asleep, she went to the window seat. With the book of shadows in her lap, she sat, staring into the falling rain.

"If I have any powers," she whispered. "Let them awaken." After all, it was the sort of language she'd heard on TV shows and read in books. If her powers would respond to anything, it would be that.

Nothing. Her body didn't glow with some long-forgotten power.

The rain began to pound, falling harder. Lightning flashed in the autumn sky, thunder hot on its heels, making the house shake.

But besides the October storm, nothing.

Lily sniffed. She wasn't a witch, then. Just a girl with a homemade book of shadows.

She tucked the book into the back of the closet as the storm, now a full-blown thunderstorm, raged on.

"Lily?" Daisy whispered. Her voice sounded small, tinny amid the pounding rain, the wind battering the house's old, drafty windows. "I'm scared."

Lily crawled into her younger sister's bed and gave her a hug. "Don't be."

"I don't like thunderstorms," she said. "Not like you do. You've always liked them."

It was true. She always had.

Lily opened her eyes, the memory falling away.

She gazed up at the ceiling of the cavern.

And then, it began to rain.

She lifted her palms upward. Her skin tingled even more.

Crackles of magic erupted on her skin, tiny balls of lightning hovering just above her palms.

A crack of thunder shook the arena.

Lily turned to Arielle. The young fae woman stepped forward, smiling. "There you have it," she said. "You're a storm witch."

"Lily?"

She turned to find Neer entering the arena, Queen Roisin at his side. He studied her with a baffled, confused look.

And then he laughed. "A storm witch. I should've known."

She frowned, the lightning disappearing, even as a few fat raindrops continued to fall. "What's that supposed to mean?"

Neer approached her, seeming undaunted by the storm of magical energy that had surrounded her only seconds before. "Storm witchcraft is a rare gift," he said. He took her hand, tracing the lines on her palm, his eyes locking with hers. "And I knew you were rare from the moment I met you. Of course such a gift would choose you."

The look in his eyes was so earnest, so sweet, that she couldn't help herself. She kissed him hard, a passionate kiss that left them both reeling.

LILY'S KISS TURNED his world sideways. She tasted like strawberries and thunder, like the wildest of magicks, and his fae magic was drawn to it.

Only the knowledge that they weren't alone and didn't have much time kept him from losing himself completely.

With a barely suppressed groan, Neer drew away.

The young fae woman, Arielle, had turned her head away, but the queen looked on, seemingly amused by their display.

She cocked her head as she studied them. "I see Arielle's magic has helped you after all. I knew it would." The queen sent the younger fae woman a look of admiration and pride.

But then, the look vanished, replaced with concern. Queen Roisin approached, all traces of amusement gone from her face.

"King Oberon sends the changeling to take young Hazel's place. Now."

"What?" Lily asked. Thunder clapped, and a few fat raindrops fell from above.

"Not yet," Roisin said, her voice, in that moment, that of a commander, a warrior queen leading her people into battle. "You must control your newly awoken magic. King Oberon is a man of a thousand curses. They walk the woods of Foster Springs. Tonight, you will make sure he doesn't visit the changeling's curse upon your daughter. Control your gift. Harness it. Wield it as though you've wielded it a thousand times before, Lily McAllister. So much is at stake for us all."

Neer saw now that though Roisin had once been foolish enough to make a deal with the unseelie king, time had made her harder, wiser.

He shivered. Years from now, Hazel would stand before this fierce queen and ask for her powers to be unbound. Roisin had explained the magic on their walk back. Even now, Neer held the amulet in his pocket. The one that would contain Hazel's powers until she was ready.

It seemed a lot to ask of his daughter—and of Rhett and Daisy's daughters. They all wanted to give the girls time to be children, time to grow before they had to face this burden. But they'd made a vow that they wouldn't lie, wouldn't shield them from what lay ahead.

Hazel and her cousins would always know about the prophecy, about their magic. But for now, Hazel's magic needed to sleep. It was the only way to ensure her safety.

And after what he'd seen tonight, he understood more than ever what was at stake. King Oberon had plans for Foster Springs—plans that went beyond that battle centuries before.

Neer was a house-elf. He understood duty. He would raise his daughter to understand it as well.

"You must go," Roisin said, a desperate edge to her voice. "Now!"

A vortex of magic grabbed them like a riptide. Neer could teleport, but the barrow was blocked and didn't allow his magic to work there. This was unlike his magic, though. It felt like he was being turned inside out.

The feeling only lasted a few seconds.

And then, he stood with Lily in Hazel's room.

"Lily!" Daisy screamed. She'd been shielding Hazel, an iron dagger in her hand. She dropped it and ran to clutch her sister. "It's outside. It's been trying to get in, searching for a way."

"Mommy! Daddy!" Hazel screamed, tears streaking her face. She leapt into Neer's arms.

He gripped her in a bear hug, not wanting to let her go. The fate of child taken by a changeling was terrible. They were trapped underground, in a constant nightmare state, while this hideous creature shapeshifted into their form, living their life.

It was the cruelest of fates. It would not be his daughter's.

The room grew quiet. There was a terrible sound—of claws scraping and scratching against the wooden siding of the farm-house.

The face of a changeling appeared in the window.

Chapter Six

*N*o. All the breath left Lily's body in a whoosh, her vision blurring. Behind her, Neer clutched Hazel in his arms their daughter's scream shattering the night.

The changeling locked eyes with Lily as it clamored into the room. Its flesh was green, its eyes glowing like embers in the night. Wind grabbed the lace curtains, sending them billowing around the creature.

Lily forced herself to meet the creature's gaze. "Leave here. Don't ever return," she growled. She clutched her hands at her side.

She felt it now—the magic, flowing in her veins. A storm witch. Between her magic and Neer's, she knew they could defend Hazel.

Beside her, Daisy stood frozen. Lily turned to her. "Take Hazel and get behind us."

Daisy shot her a look that said she thought her sister was out of her mind, but she did.

"My daddy has magic, so you better run!" Hazel shouted.

Lily couldn't help but admire her daughter's courage.

She is so much braver than I've ever been, Lily thought.

"I don't care about your daddy's magic," the changeling hissed. "I care about yours. King Oberon himself wants to meet you." Nothing about that statement sounded pleasant.

An energy ball shot through the room, a ball of blue magic that hit the changeling square in the chest, knocking it back into the wall. That blast was no doubt courtesy of her husband, who obviously didn't care for the changeling addressing his daughter.

Neer stepped forward. "Stay away from my daughter."

The changeling shook off the blow. It shouldn't have been able to, but it did. The creature rose on surprisingly steady feet.

"The king gave me an extra dose of magic, house-elf."

Crap. Neer's energy balls took a lot of his magic. He wouldn't be able to launch another one for several hours. Most house-elves' magic was more about shielding than actual defensive magic. That was the one arrow in Neer's magical quiver—and the changeling knew it. But there was one thing it didn't know.

Lily tilted her head skyward. The ceiling was dotted with glow-in-the-dark stars in the shape of a spiral, but she imagined past that.

Instead, she imagined herself on a mountaintop, looking down on the woods full of malicious fae. She called to the storm that waited in the sky above.

Magic built up, a feeling of static and tingles in her hands. She opened her hands and smiled at the creature.

"You should've left when you had the chance." She launched the ball of lightning in her right hand first, then the one in her left.

The changeling's scream was ear-piercing. It was a cry of pain.

The smell of charred flesh and singed hair filled the room as the creature wailed. A gale-force wind slammed into the house, knocking over a lamp.

Lily knew she needed to press pause on her magic before she brought the house down around them. She grounded herself, as she had a thousand times before. She'd always thought the simple ritual of grounding was something she needed because of anxiety or her restless nature.

It had never occurred to her she would need it to ground her magic.

She knelt, placing her hands on the hardwood floor, imagining herself rooted in the cool, fertile earth, the scent of her garden around her.

She felt large hands come to rest on her shoulders. Neer, standing behind her, lending her his calming energy, his grounding presence.

When she was sure the magical storm within her had dissipated, she opened her eyes and turned behind her.

Daisy was looking at her like...well, still like she thought Lily had lost her mind. Hazel was curled against her aunt, wiggling out of her grasp.

"Mommy!" Hazel exclaimed. "Do you have magic?"

Lily smiled. She crossed the room and swept her daughter into her arms while Neer covered the changeling with a blanket. There would be a lot of protective spells and cleansing rituals cast over this room in the days to come.

"I do, my love." She kissed Hazel's forehead and brushed her tangled hair away from her face. "I do."

Hazel squirmed, craning her head to meet her mother's eyes. "We all have magic? All three of us?"

"We do," Lily said. Behind her, Neer cleared his throat. They had to tell her, and they both knew it. "Hazel, about your magic..."

Hazel frowned. "The bad faerie wanted it."

"Yes. We have to hide it away for a while, keep it safe. Not forever."

Her daughter's frown deepened. "For how long?"

Lily smoothed her daughter's hair, blinking away tears. "Until you're all grown up."

"That will take forever," Hazel said. "What if I learn to protect myself? I can make lightning. Or wind. Or storms. Or an army of fireflies..."

Lily sat on the floor and tugged Hazel into her lap. Neer sat beside them. The wind was a gentle breeze now, carrying on it the sound of gentle rain left behind in the wake of Lily's magic.

Neer pulled out an amulet, the stone delicate purple. Amethyst—one of Lily's favorites. He held it out, letting it dangle on its silver chain.

"Someday you will learn to do all of those things," he said to their daughter. "And so many more. You will do great things with your magic. But right now, your magic needs to sleep. It will be waiting for you."

"No more fireflies?" Hazel sobbed.

Lily's heart broke for her daughter. She had a gift, but it was being taken away.

But it was the only way to keep Hazel safe. Lily couldn't protect Hazel forever—but for now, she could do this.

"There is a faerie queen, my love, and she needs your help," Neer said. "Come on. Let's sit outside and I'll tell you all about it."

He picked Hazel up, and they all went outside, sitting on the covered back porch, the rain a gentle backdrop. They wrapped a quilt around themselves.

Daisy went to call Rhett and fill him in on what had happened, her eyes brimming with questions waiting to be answered.

And then, they tucked Hazel between them, letting her hold and admire the amethyst amulet while Neer told her the story. He made it sound beautiful and wondrous, and Lily knew he left out some of the worst details.

Hazel couldn't possibly know how this particular faerie tale would shape her life. But she peppered her father with questions as he spoke, leaning her body against his.

By the end, sleep overcame curiosity, and she fell asleep, the amulet in her hands.

Neer tugged it out of Hazel's loose grasp, holding it up to examine it. The purple stone glittered in the shadows, shimmering with the glow of Hazel's magic.

An ache formed in Lily's chest.

"She won't remember tonight?" Lily asked.

"The queen assured me she wouldn't. We can tell her she has magic, of course, but tonight will be like a forgotten dream." Neer squeezed Lily's shoulder. "It's for the best."

"I know," Lily said with a nod.

The amulet glowed, shimmers of silvery light appearing around it. And then it disappeared—back to the queen's barrow, where it would wait with the others, until the sisters were ready.

They tucked Hazel into their bed, and then Lily put on the kettle. Daisy waited in the living room, flipping through an old seed catalog and twisting in her seat, obviously impatient for answers.

Lily filled a teapot with chocolate mint tea. She placed the pot and a few cups, along with a bar of dark chocolate and a few shortbread cookies, on a tray.

Neer entered the kitchen.

"Hazel's still fast asleep," he assured her.

He opened his arms to her, and she flew into his embrace.

As always, it felt like coming home. He was her rock through all of life's storms—even if some of those storms were of her own mystical making.

Neer tightened his arms around her. "You and Hazel," he began. He cleared his throat. "You are my whole world."

Lily smiled, resting her cheek against his chest. "Even if you do wonder sometimes what you got yourself into?"

"That's half the fun," he said. "And now we know how you managed to summon me that night all those years ago."

She laughed, remembering. "A storm witch. Who would've thought?"

He chuckled, the sound warm, like hot tea on a cold night. "In hindsight, there were signs," he teased.

Lily drew away, buoyed by his presence, knowing whatever they faced, they faced together.

"Well, we'd better go tell my sister what's going on."

"Yeah, I think she has a few questions for you. Maybe this is a, uh, sisters-only sort of deal?" he said.

Lily nodded, scooping up the tray. "Yeah, I think so. Go stay with Hazel."

He kissed her goodnight, and headed upstairs.

Lily plopped the tray down on the coffee table in the living room, where Daisy waited on the sofa.

"Tell me everything," Daisy said, leaning forward.

Lily poured the tea.

And then, she did, in fact, tell her sister everything.

I hope you enjoyed reading the Faerie Spells Series. If you're interested in a free short story, visit www.denisedyoungbooks.com/ newsletter and sign up to receive a free copy of Fractured Moonlight, *a stand-alone short story that's equal parts fairy tale and sweet romance.*

Looking for a slightly steamier read filled with tarot cards, romance, and witchcraft? Turn the page to read a sneak peek of Tangled Roots, *the first book in the Witches of Willow Creek: Tangled Magic Paranormal Romance Series.*

About the Author

E qual parts bookworm, flower child, and eclectic witch, Denise D. Young writes fantasy and paranormal romance featuring witches, magic, faeries, and the occasional shifter.

Denise lives with her husband and their animals in the mountains of Virginia. She reads tarot cards, collects crystals, gazes at stars, and believes magic is the answer (no matter what the question was).

If you've ever hoped to find a book of spells in a dusty attic, if you suspect every misty forest contains a hidden portal to another realm, or if you don't mind a little darkness before your happily-ever-after, her books might be just the thing you've been waiting for.

Find Denise on her web home at www.denisedyoungbooks.com or connect with her on facebook.com/denisedyoungbooks.
For a complete list of all of Denise's books and series, visit www.denisedyoungbooks.com/booklist.

A Sneak Peek of Tangled Roots (Witches of Willow Creek: Tangled Magic #1)

Tangled Roots: Prologue

CASSIE
Willow Creek, Virginia: 1974

There was wildness in the air.

I tipped my head back, breathing it in. The languid summer heat hit my bare throat.

Mine, the magic whispered.

Yes, my soul whispered back. *Yes, all things wild and sacred, all things born of the goddess's womb.*

Yes.

Long blond hair fell across my face. I untied the swath of white ribbon fastened at my throat and secured it in a loose ponytail at my nape.

My hand shook as I withdrew it, damp with moisture from the back of my neck.

It was the summer heat, I reasoned. Nothing more.

Not Nathan's letter, not the memory of his harsh, accusatory voice.

Not the dreams that followed, the fear that I'd turn a corner or open a door and see my hulking brother's form looming over me.

Not the words he'd written that were seared into my brain—words that others might take as a plea but I knew to be a command.

Come home.

The tremors raked my body again, an old fear of magic caged.

Willow Creek was home. My coven was home. Buttercup Diner, where I waited tables and wiped greasy hands on my red apron, that was home.

That little white house in the Georgia mountains, where I could look at the forest but never enter it? That attic bedroom where magic stalked inside my soul like a carnival's caged lion, muscles primed but never able to pounce, aching for release?

That was not home.

I'd watched the Summer of Love and Woodstock come and go. I'd watched both the upheaval and freedom. But I'd been a bystander. In this world. In my life.

I wasn't anymore.

Nathan would make me one again.

My breath quickened.

I didn't know how my brother found me—didn't care. I hadn't thought he or my parents cared enough to look. But I knew Nathan was on a mission from Mama, and that meant soon enough he'd be pounding at my door.

I smoothed my damp palm across the cotton fabric of my knee-length eyelet dress—handmade. Continuing to make my clothes by hand was one of the few remnants of home I allowed myself. The whir of the sewing machine, its rhythm a reassuring beat. The tug of needle and thread until my fingers bled.

Good discipline, my father said.

Keeps her mind off things, Mama always agreed.

Just because the world's gone to hell in a handbasket doesn't mean you have to.

Nathan's words, pounding in my head. I burnt the letter before one of my coven-sisters could see it. I spoke words of release, trying to free myself from the past.

It wasn't enough.

I could feel the blood that connected us, pulling me toward him—toward my past.

And from my fear, this spell emerged.

If I dug deep enough in my magic, I could summon the Guardian of Willow Creek, Virginia. She could block Nathan's path.

She could stop him from dragging me back to that place where I was barely half-alive.

I exhaled, the sound almost sharp in the sleepy forest, the way a drop of water in a cave is magnified.

Ginny, my high priestess, my mentor, was back at the farmhouse she called home, a scant half-mile hike across wooded hills and neatly tended rows of crops. She'd been at her sketchpad when I left her house, her blond hair in a careless braid as she drew the pattern for her next quilt.

Her eyes locked with mine for a split second, a glint of caution in them. "Be careful."

I'd felt her gaze on me as the screen door squeaked shut behind me.

I felt it still, the magic of the coven a thread gently tugging on my own magic.

I pressed my palms to rich, dark soil. I knelt against the forest floor, not caring about the stains on my dress.

Inhale. Balmy summer night, scent of sunbaked earth and Virginia pine.

Exhale. Release the past.

Open my eyes. Look forward.

I struck a match, hand's tremble lessened now but still there. The scent of freshly struck sulfur stung my nostrils. Upon the matchhead danced a wisp of a magical creature, its body living flame—salamander, elemental of fire.

I pressed the match to the waiting black votive candle, made by one of my coven sisters, Tricia, and watched as the flame took root on the wick. The salamander stretched out tiny arms, dancing—beauty, magic, fire personified.

"Bless this space, element of fire," I whispered to her.

I took up a feather, one I found shortly after the summer solstice. Ginny told me it was from a barred owl. "The barred owl is a familiar of the Guardian," Ginny remarked. "She's got a close eye on you." Serious, those words—and her tone a little curious.

I moved the feather up, down, diagonal, forming the shape of a pentacle in the air.

"Bless this space, element of air." I felt, not saw, the moment the sylph arrived—for air was my element, my magic. A witch could work with any elemental magic, of course, but she—or he—always had a close affinity for one. Air was mine.

The sylph hovered behind me, the beat of her wings stirring the air, but she didn't show herself. "Caution, lovely witch. There are silver wisps of magic stirring around you this night. What you work brings deep change. Tread lightly."

Magic tingled across my skin like falling glitter, and then I felt her retreat.

Riddles. Elementals, when they spoke at all to mere mortals, always spoke in riddles.

Next, I took out a small mason jar and poured the water in a slow circle around the lit candle, careful not to disturb the flame, though the salamander had vanished back to her realm. The water was from Willow Creek, which formed the westernmost boundary of Ginny's farm, and for which the town itself was named.

"Bless this space, element of water." None of the undine appeared, and I didn't expect them to, though sometimes I heard a hint of their song drifting on the air.

But only silence reached my ears this night.

I shook away the sense of foreboding. It was only the rising magic, I reasoned, that made the temperature seem to drop. It was only my lingering concern over Nathan's letter that made my stomach queasy.

Without looking, I reached into the familiar wicker basket and withdrew the last item—the most important.

Earth.

The Guardian of Willow Creek was at her heart a being of earth. That much I knew, though I knew little else about her—save that she was powerful, temperamental, and did not suffer fools.

Was I such a fool?

Ginny's warnings about the Guardian almost stilled my hand, but I clutched the bag of silvery green moss harder. There was no going back. Not now, after two years of freedom. I'd run from home the night of my high school graduation, buying a bus ticket to New York City with money saved up from some sewing jobs I'd done for Mama's friends.

New York City, I figured, was as far away from that little farmhouse as I could get. It was a big enough place to vanish into the crowds. And in that anonymity, I'd reasoned, I could find freedom.

Turned out, I found it in this small Virginia town instead.

And I'd risk the Guardian's wrath before I'd risk being dragged backward.

I carefully encircled the black votive with the moss, pressing it against the waiting earth. Tendrils of magic snaked into the earth, in hues of amber brown and leafy green.

"Bless this space, element of earth."

"A witch in time saves nine."

I smirked slightly at the gnome's garbled rendition of the familiar phrase. "A *stitch* in time saves nine," I corrected.

"Not this time." There's a gentle rustle, and I feel the elementals, having blessed the space, all retreat.

Inhale.

The scent of earth was heavy now, even for the forest. Maidenhair fern's spice. Mushrooms pungent aroma. Damp stone's musty scent.

The ground underneath me seemed to tilt and sway.

I rose on unsteady feet. An unseen force slammed me in the tree behind me.

I crumpled against the thick trunk, stars dancing in my vision. The candle went out.

I fell, though I was already lying on the forest floor. The ground gave way, and I fell.

TORCHES' FLAMES DANCED. Above me, quartz crystal points in their many forms—clear as glass, smoky gray, the yellow of citrine, the purple of amethyst and pale pink of rose quartz—jutted from the earth below and cavernous ceiling above. Silver moss dangled. The eyes of unseen creatures peered from the shadows, hidden by swirling silvery mists.

The mists before me parted, revealing a throne carved of dark, twisting wood, as though the tree from which it was carved were still alive, still sentient, still growing. Green crystals poked out here and there. Behind it was a wall of dark green vines speckled with red roses the size of small cabbages.

But it was the figure who sat in that throne—and such a chair could only rightly be called a throne—who sent my jaw dropping.

"Cassandra Anne Gearhart." Full lips, a deep, plum purple, almost black but glistening as though they'd kissed the stars, turned upward in a dark, sinister smile as they hissed my name.

I stepped backward, but a wall of vines pressed against me, halting any retreat. "Yes?"

Her eyes were silver like the mists, but bright as the coldest of winter stars. Her skin was bronze as though stained with earth, her hair a twisting mass of light brown braids filled with moss and twigs.

She rose. I was short—a mere five-foot—so most people seemed tall to me, but she was purely a giantess. She towered over me, her robes the same near-black purple of her lips, threaded with green, amber, and teal threads. I almost reached out to caress the billowing fabric, to test its fibers under my fingers. Instead, I curled my fingers into my palms.

She reached out with bony fingers and tilted my head upwards, until I strained backwards to meet her glinting gaze.

That smile again. Wise and wicked. "I will grant your wish."

"You'll..." I sucked in my lips. It was too easy. I shouldn't have done this. "You'll make sure Nathan can't find me."

She nodded, each bob of her head deliberate, decisive. "Yes. But there's a price."

"What would you ask of me?" The words came out a little too high, too desperate. Never a good position when one was facing such a powerful being.

"I see far more than you, and I am not obligated to tell you all that I see," she snapped.

I lowered my gaze back to the wall of vines. "Of course, my lady."

She released my chin from her bony clutches, and I sighed with relief. "One day, you will awaken. You will sleep for many years, and, when I need you, you will awaken."

"I don't understand. How does that stop...How does that grant my wish?"

A gust of wind shook the cavern. "I do *not* owe little mortals explanations." She tilted her head, as if listen to whispers the wind carried. "He's here, you know. Your father is sick. Do you want to go home?"

"I want to stay in Willow Creek."

"Then you'll stay. I can make that so. Do you agree to my terms?"

"I don't understand your terms." I inhaled, wishing I could suck the words back in, swallow them.

To my surprise, she chuckled. "You don't need to. If I release you this night without granting your wish, he will find you. Or you can accept my offer. But I'm not a creature of patience, immortal though I might be."

That attic bedroom. Those woods I couldn't enter.

What fate could be worse than magic caged?

"I accept."

She nodded. "Then as I will it, so mote it be."

Ribbons of magic twisted in the air, wrapping around me, tugging me back up through the earth.

"I know she's here, bitch!" My blood ran cold at those words. I tried to crane my head, to see where Nathan's voice came from, but every muscle was stiff, frozen.

"Don't you dare speak to me that way. Get off my land. This is private property." Ginny's voice, madder than I'd ever heard her.

Nathan came into view. He'd grown a beard since last I saw him, and even in the moonlight I could see how red his face was. "Where is she? Cassandra? Cassie!"

I'd seen my brother angry before and, not for the first time, I feared that in his rage he'd hurt me. I tried to run, but my feet were rooted to the earth.

He glared down at the candle, pointing at the now extinguished flame. The spell was over, the magic cast.

What had I done wrong? Why hadn't she saved me?

Why couldn't I run?

Ginny got in Nathan's path, blocking him. She was tall for a woman and matched his height. "Boy, unless you want an ass full of birdshot, get off my farm. Do you hear me?"

Nathan strode off into the woods, calling my name. Why hadn't he seen me? I was standing right in front of him.

The tension in me eased as he stomped off, the sound of him yelling my name growing more distant.

Ginny knelt down and picked up a handful of moss and the owl feather. She shifted them from palm to palm, as if testing the weight of the spell's remnants in her hands. "Cassie. Miss Cassie, what have you gone and done?"

She gasped. Her eyes flew open, the moss tumbling down, the feather fluttering toward the ground. She spun to face me. She reached out and raked her hands against my cheek, but her touch was distant, as though through layer upon layer of papier-mâché. "Oh, child, sweet Cassie. Why has she done this to you?"

I tried to speak, to ask her what she meant. I tried to shift my weight, to meet her gaze. Nothing. I was rooted.

Then I realized.

I was, indeed, rooted in the earth.

A tree. The Guardian had made me a tree.

I tried to open my mouth to scream.

All those years, my magic trapped inside.

And now, again, in my haste to maintain freedom, I was trapped again.

Tangled Roots **is now available!**